Delusion for a Lonely Girl

Sylvia Nickels

ISBN-978-0-9799222-4-4
ISBN-0-9799222-4-0

Interior Design: Sylvia Nickels
Cover Design: Sylvia Nickels

A Different Drummer Publishing

First edition of Delusion for a Lonely Girl was published by Oconee Spirit Press 2016

Acknowledgments

To everyone who has encouraged me all through the years to keep pursuing my dream of publication, my heartfelt thanks. I have been so fortunate to have the steadfast support of my immediate and extended family as well as the many talented writers in my writing groups. Their critiques and suggestions have been on point. If my books have any merit, it is most likely because of that support and those suggestions. Their acceptance of me as a bona fide writer gave me that much-sought-after prize of all writers, validation as a writer.

One

The only sound in my office was gurgling water in the fifty gallon aquarium that sat oa credenza with several wide drawers. Two powerful pumps circulated water through the aquarium though it held no fin-tailed residents. The credenza and aquarium filled the window alcove to my right as I sat at my desk, which faced the outside door to my home office. Concealed lighting illuminated luxurious, lacy green landscapes and shadowy grottoes. During the day, light from the windows was multiplied by the huge tank and gave the room a light and airy feel. At night or on overcast days, the bubbling water caused the tank lights to pulse through the darkness and cast a pleasing green ambiance over the room.

I pulled out receipts and my notebook, pulled up an invoice form in Open Office and input a few lines. My eyes kept straying to the big television screen mounted on the wall in front of me. The set was on any time I was in the office, but with the sound muted. I reached for the remote and when a picture of the Tennessee State Attorney General came up, I hit the sound button. The news anchor's voiceover was reporting the formation of a federal, multi-state and local Task Force. The Task Force was charged with purging Tennessee and surrounding southern states of the connected crimes of illegal drugs and human trafficking.

I knew the AG by sight, of course. When the camera drew back and the picture widened out, I recognized another person. Taylor Glass, Special Agent with the TBI, was standing with several other members of the newly formed task force. I'd met Taylor last year when we'd both been involved in the case that almost ended my life and did end Dan Traynor's sojourn on earth.

I wasn't surprised that she was involved in this Task Force. She seemed on the fast track for advancement up the ranks of the state's top police agency. When the other names on the roster for the Task Force were given, I recognized another one, Detective Sergeant Jake Hunter, with the Roswell, Georgia Police Department.

Coming up in the world, Jake.

I'd met Jake years ago when my first husband was killed while being held in jail on a domestic complaint I'd filed. Jake had unofficially looked into my mother's death in a car crash, which I suspected my stepfather had engineered. And along with Taylor Glass last year, Jake came back into my life when my second abusive husband, by then ex, was identified as a sibling of one of two women murder victims. And then my ex also became a victim. I can really pick husbands.

"About time," I muttered, meaning the Task Force. Several news stories over the last year had aired about young people of both sexes, even some children, being found with degenerates who forced them into porn and sex slavery. In one local case the low-life was actually the mother of the four girls.

The final sound byte went to the AG. "Victims fear violence to themselves or their families if they speak up. People who want to prey on them see these victims as vulnerable. We are going to stop this. Local departments, with some Federal financial help, will provide victims with highly trained counselors, sexual assault resources and case advocates."

A few months earlier Detective Sergeant Shac Lane and his partner had been sent to a seminar in Nashville which focused on the subject of human trafficking. Officers from every jurisdiction across the state were eager to attend. Shac said they were told at the time a task force to combat the sex crimes was in the works.

When he came back we discussed what they'd been taught at the seminar. A lot I knew just from the news and talking to Shac about what he'd learned on the job. But I did not know the actual hideous scope of it all.

"They aim to arm frontline police officers with training to recognize signs of sex trafficking," he told me over coffee in my kitchen the day after he returned to Wexler Bend from Nashville. "Most of the time human trafficking doesn't exist in a vacuum, nor just within a county or a city."

"Can't it be spotted? What about that couple selling their daughters for porn films?"

"Tip of the iceberg, Cam. We'll jail a prostitute and let her out the next morning. On the surface she may be viewed as the perpetrator. But she can just as likely be a victim."

I nodded, remembering my work at the women's shelter, I knew how women could be beaten down and accept any abasement from a man just to keep him.

"The seminar instructed us to learn to dig deeper," Shac said, "figure out if there might be a wider criminal operation going on."

I wished the Task Force spectacular success in stopping the trafficking, muted the television again and got back to work completing and printing invoices. I addressed and preprinted postage on half a dozen envelopes then stuffed the completed invoices in them.

Glad to finally stand up after sitting for several hours, I had car keys in hand and was headed for the door when my phone rang, the office line. I considered letting the answering machine get it but turned back and picked up the receiver.

Two

"Is this Cameron Locke?" The voice sounded hesitant and I got the impression she had almost hung up after just one ring.

"Yes. Can I help you?"

"I – I'm not sure. You're a private detective?"

"I am."

The line was silent for a long time and I wondered if she had hung up after all. Then she spoke again, her voice stronger. "What exactly do you do?"

I thought she was stalling for time, trying to make up her mind. And I remembered some of the calls when I worked for Dan Traynor to qualify for my own license. I'd get impatient sometimes when potential clients dithered before they got to the point. I could almost hear his gentle voice repeating what he'd told me then.

"Patience, Cam," he'd caution me. "By the time someone thinks they need a PI, they've most likely been through some type of emotional trauma. Give them time to decide to trust you."

I took a deep breath, tried to think what might reassure this hesitant young woman, her voice sounded young anyway. "I do a lot of searching through records to locate information and to find whatever a client might want found."

"I – I just want to know he's all right." She said in a rush.

"Would you like to make an appointment?" I glanced at my desk calendar.

"Could you see me today?"

"I'm just leaving on an errand for an hour or so. Say two-thirty?"

"All right. I'll be there."

"You know where my office is located?"

"The newspaper said you're at Wexler Pointe Condos, right?"

Apparently she'd found me through the archived story the Wexler Bend newspaper had run about the case that occasioned my near-death experience. "No. I've moved." I gave her my new address and told her to come to the side entrance of the house.

I returned from the post office about two-fifteen to see a late-model Infiniti parked on the gravel area next to the driveway. By the time I'd got my key in the door she had walked up behind me. She was young, not as young as she sounded, but still very young. Maybe eighteen, possibly nineteen. Her short skirt and dark patterned tights made me think she might be a student at the community college. But the designer scarf and her jewelry was not the usual student getup. A blonde Barbie Doll version of a college student.

We went inside and I punched in the alarm code on the keypad beside the door. She moved immediately to the aquarium and stared, probably looking for the fish like most people who came into the office.

"They all died." I said, not caring to go into the reason. Dan had loved tropical fish but stopped trying to keep them when twice they all died while he was on an extended stakeout.

"Oh." She turned away and walked to the client chair beside my desk. She clasped her hands in a death grip on her Coach purse straps.

I picked up a pen and pulled a pad forward as I sat down. "May I have your name?"

"Anything I tell you will be kept confidential, won't it?" She kept twisting the straps of the purse.

"Unless your case becomes a criminal matter and I'm required to divulge it to the police, yes."

Blonde hair swung across her face as she looked down at her lap. For the first time I realized the hair was a wig. A high dollar wig, which was why I hadn't identified it as one at first. When I did, I figured she'd give a fictitious name.

"Ummm. It's Mindy Clark." She paused and swallowed.

Okay. I'd have to get her real name another way. "And you need my services because - ?"

"My boyfriend has disappeared."

"You know he's disappeared? He isn't at his home? Haven't been able to reach him by phone?" I didn't want to offend her by assuming they lived together in case they didn't.

"I went to his apartment. Several times. He doesn't answer. The last time I was there, I talked to one of the neighbors who said he'd never even seen or heard of anyone by that name living there. And no, he doesn't answer his phone. Calls go straight to voice mail and I've left dozens of messages, but he hasn't returned them."

"You're close, I take it? Usually see each other regularly?"

"Oh, yes. He helps me with my classes. I have trouble understanding some of the material."

"What's your major?"

"Poli sci."

Not her original major, I was willing to bet. I would have pegged her as pursuing one of those 'fill-in-the-blank Appreciation' majors with zero application to the real world. Given her designer outfit, at least half carat diamond ear studs below two gold ones and the quarter carat gem stuck in the right side of her nose, her parents had more money than time for her. She'd probably changed majors because of her boyfriend. Maybe an older student and she'd followed him to Wexler Bend Community College. I'd wound up here because of a man, too. She didn't sound like a Tennessee native. Her accent placed her origins as further South, Georgia or Alabama.

"Did you transfer from another college? Did he? Or did you meet him here?"

"My parents insisted I transfer when Southern Moldings moved Dad here." She paused a second, and a look of chagrin passed over her face. She'd realized she might have given away her identity. "I wasn't very happy about it, I wanted to stay in – where we were - until I met Whitt."

So her father worked for my old company, with its new name. In management. Shouldn't be too hard to get his name. The company merger was one reason I was now a private eye, I'd lost my job as head of security for Eastern Fabricators. I'm not complaining now that I'm semi-established in the profession. I'm my own boss and can choose my cases. But since I like to eat, I can't be too choosy, of course.

"Is Whitt a classmate?" I asked. Unhappy young women sometimes choose boyfriends unwisely. As I well knew.

She fiddled with the clasp on her purse. "No. I met him at the Campus Coffee Shop a week ago."

Another lie. She'd known him longer than a week, I'd bet a month's income on it. Which was not a lot of money, but more than I could afford to lose.

"He bought me a latte and we clicked. He's been active in civic organizations, even served as an alderman for a year, he said. He made it sound exciting so I switched my major from fashion design to poli sci."

"When did you see Whitt last? And did he say anything about a trip?"

"Oh, no. And he would have. We had planned to spend the weekend in Gatlinburg. Our first weekend together."

"I'll need his full name, address, make of car, workplace, and so on, then I'll see if I can track him down. You said on the phone you just want to know he's okay. You don't want him to know you're looking for him?"

"No, certainly not." For the first time she showed the animation usually associated with her age. "I don't want him to think I'm chasing him!"

"Right. Okay. I'll just see if I can locate him, let you know and you take it from there."

When I mentioned that I usually required at least a two hundred dollar retainer, she didn't bat an eye. She peeled two hundred dollar bills from a roll she pulled from her purse.

Daughters of management at Southern Molding must receive hefty allowances. Designer clothes and wigs, Coach purses, wads of cash. Not to mention a new Infiniti. Or she and Whitt were involved in more than romance. I mentally slapped myself. Stop jumping to conclusions. Your envy is showing.

I gave her a receipt and she was ready to bolt. I managed to detain her long enough to get Whitt's address, description and approximate age. She thought he was close to her age, but I knew better if he told her the truth about having served as an alderman. He had to be at least twenty-eight, the minimum age in Wexler Bend to qualify. And a little long in the tooth to be hanging around a campus coffee shop. My finely-honed-by-experience antenna for picking up predators on the prowl was pinging. But why hadn't he hung around?

She practically ran to her car, as anxious to leave as she had initially been to see me, it seemed.

Three

After she left I entered the details, such as they were, into a file on my computer. I clicked on the link to a database that listed more information about movers and shakers in the business world than they cared for the world to know. But in this modern world of instant communication, privacy is a lost commodity. I was stopped on the first page, however, by a curt notice that I had failed to renew my membership on the site.

"Rats."

I clicked on the renewal box, but received another notice that the site was down for a few hours for routine maintenance and updating.

"Double rats."

So I surfed over to the City of Wexler Bend website and then the archives to see if it had a list of former aldermen. Nope. Just current pols who supposedly wanted to do their civic duty. Nothing to do with wanting access to inside information and getting contracts for future city projects. Perish the thought.

The archive for the *Wexler Bend Chronicle* past issues was my next virtual destination. No hits for articles about any alderman with the first name of Whitt came up. Maybe my lack of expectation was to blame. But after searching several more possible websites including the World Wide Web itself, I still came up blank.

So I switched to searching for any references to Southern Moldings. Not surprisingly the company was listed on the New York Stock Exchange. Since I was not knowledgeable about stocks, I didn't know if the share price was good, bad or indifferent. I found a few news stories, most in the newspaper in the town where the company was headquartered, New Corners, Alabama. So my guess as to where Mindy, if that was her name, and her family had moved from to Wexler Bend must be accurate. I'd have to wait until I could access the management database to get their real name.

Unless. I knew a few people who had been retained from Eastern Fabricators when Southern Moldings took over. I checked my old-fashioned Rolodex and found the number for Maxie Filner. She'd been head of the accounting department for Eastern and taken a demotion to keep a job. A single mom with three children, I could hardly blame her. Maxie should be home by now since the clock showed five minutes after five. She got off at four-thirty. If she was making dinner, I wouldn't hold her long.

I could hear loud kid noises when Maxie picked up the phone.

"Maxie, this is Cam Locke. I can call back if this is a bad time."

"It's okay. Let me get out of the kitchen. I picked up pizzas and the kids are arguing over who got the biggest slice."

I heard the sound of a door closing and the kid voices grew more muffled. "How are you, Cam? I heard you're a PI now."

"Yep. For good or ill. How are you doing? Southern Moldings treating you all right?"

"All right, I guess. Their imported accountants don't really seem to understand the difference in a debit and credit, but other than that, it's a job." Her laugh sounded a little brittle.

"Seems like they imported most of their employees as well as management. I wondered if you could give me a little information about a management import."

She was quiet for several seconds. I hastened to add, "Just a name, no actual information. Did they bring top management from New Corners? I know the new Security Chief was from there."

"Yes, the First Vice President is, too. They're of well-heeled Hispanic origin, I've heard. Also that the wife and seventeen-year-old daughter, she'd be eighteen now, weren't too keen to move to the mountains. He usually only comes around at the end of the quarter."

"Who in the world wouldn't want to come to these beautiful mountains?" I laughed. "Of course, there's not much to do except hobnob with the local elite at Clare View. What's their name?"

"The Robert Gorens. I understand they hobnob, all right." I heard a stifled giggle. "Seems almost as if he's taken Taggert's place as the company drunk. Did you see the small notice in the Chronicle when he was charged with DUI?"

"No, I didn't. When?"

"Month or so ago. I'm not surprised even you didn't hear about it. The company was able to get it hushed up and any other publicity quashed."

We chatted for a few minutes until apparently a door opened and a kid screamed bloody murder, though I couldn't understand the words.

"Gotta go and see who's killing who, Cam. Let's go out to lunch soon." Maxie hung up.

Four

The young girl drove aimlessly for a couple of hours. She knew she had to replace the money she'd taken from the roll of bills. How? She shifted position and her waistband caught on the diamond piercing in her navel. It had to be worth way more than two hundred dollars. Dusk was falling as she drove along an unfamiliar street that led out of town. After a mile or so it narrowed to two lanes. Before she got lost she probably should turn back toward town where she'd be more apt to find a pawn shop.

Just then she saw a run-down shopping center on the left. A sign flashed the word 'PAWN' in red neon in a shop window on the end. She pulled the Infinity into the potholed parking lot. As she left the car she heard paper rustle in her pocket. She pulled out the receipt from the private detective. The woman had given her both copies, not just the original. She threw the papers on the floor of the car. In her anxiety to replace the two hundred dollars she didn't notice one of the copies drift almost under the seat.

The man in the pawn shop wouldn't give her two hundred for the navel diamond. She argued, but he was adamant.

"One fifty, take it or leave it."

She knew he could see she was desperate so she finally agreed. Stuffing the money in her purse, she returned to the car.

She gripped the wheel and tried to calm herself before turning the ignition key. She usually enjoyed driving the car because it practically drove itself. Her mom wouldn't let her drive her old Caddy. She wished her snooty classmates or always-angry mother could see her at the wheel of this car. They'd be so envious.

Her trips on Interstate highways were pure pleasure. Well, almost. She pushed away the thought of what she had to do when she arrived in Georgia and Alabama. Her throat hurt and she gagged at the memory.

A soft ping sounded and she looked at the displays on her dashboard. The tiny icon of a gas tank and another ping alerted her to the fact that she was very low on gasoline. Better stop at the next station. As if in answer to the thought a brightly-lit service station and convenience store came into view on the right side of the road.

She should have noticed the low fuel level. She had to meet the man in the ski mask at ten the next morning. And she needed to take more of the anti-nausea liquid as soon as she got home. She hoped her parents would be at the country club. Her dad would probably be almost passed out drunk when they finally left the club. Her mother would be screaming at him as soon as they came in.

"Why must you always humiliate me? Why oh why did I marry a man who can't hold his liquor?"

Her dad would mumble something about needing to lie down.

"Oh, yes. Sleep it off. And when you wake up you won't remember spilling your drink down the front of my dress. With everyone trying to act like they didn't notice."

The shouting would go on for hours, as usual.

Neither parent paid much attention to what she did. Whitt was different. He treated her like an adult. Told her he went by that other name she'd heard someone call him at the party so people wouldn't try to con him out of drugs.

Where was he? Why had he abandoned her, too? He'd said he loved her. He'd said they'd go to Gatlinburg for a weekend, she'd have him all to herself. He promised he'd break off his engagement soon. Then they could be seen together openly.

The man in the ski mask said this would be the last transport she'd have to make. Then her dad's job would be safe, his debt paid off. She hated what she'd had to do to protect her family. Wanted to hate her father for being the cause, his drinking and gambling. But she blamed her mother the most. She could never be satisfied with the money he made, the house they lived in. Always wanting more. Wanting to keep up with the people they met at country clubs and expensive social affairs.

She pulled in to the second unoccupied pump and pulled out her debit card. The card reader wouldn't accept the card. She was afraid to use any more of the roll of money. She walked into the station to complain about the card reader, detoured down a candy aisle when she realized she was hungry.

A man stood in the aisle perusing the snack cracker display. She grabbed his arm with a happy smile, "Whitt? You're all right! Why didn't you answer your phone or call me back?"

Whitt looked startled, then a weak smile replaced it. "Hey, Baby. I've been busy." He almost whispered.

"I need to talk to you." She leaned against him. "I've been so worried."

"Let's get out of here. In your car."

"I'm almost out of gas and for some reason the pump won't take my debit card."

He put a twenty in her hand. "Here. Use this. I'll wait in your car." He was gone before she could respond.

She went to the clerk and handed her the twenty, told her the pump number. When she reached her car, Whitt was slumped in the passenger seat and didn't offer to pump her gas.

When she'd pumped the twenty dollars worth of gas in her tank she replaced the hose and got in on the driver's side. She resisted the urge to complain about his thoughtlessness. He was now wearing gloves though it was a warm night, but she didn't ask why. He was acting so strange. She just wanted things to be the way they had been, wanted him to kiss her, tell her how pretty she was. She pushed away thoughts of that party with just him and two other men. One turned out to be the ski mask man. Whitt insisted she be 'nice' to them. She felt so dirty afterward.

She realized he was talking to her. "We're near the river. Take the next left and drive a quarter mile. There's a cleared area, used to be an old mill."

Without saying anything she did as he instructed. A bit of light remained in the sky when they arrived at the old mill site. He opened the door, got out of the car and started walking toward the river. She trotted to catch up with him. "Whitt. What's wrong?"

"I can't see you anymore. I hoped you'd get the message when I didn't return your calls."

She fell back and tears streamed from her eyes. "Wh-What? How can you say that? We love each other."

He turned on her, savage words erupting. "You think because your father's a vice president of a company that your family and background don't matter? He's a token to political correctness. Always has been just a token. You should know that and keep your place."

She flailed out in pain, hitting him on the arm, in the chest, trying to defend her family. "You're lying. Why are you saying that?" Her voice was broken by sobs.

"It made me sick the way we set you up like some kind of princess. The clothes, the jewelry, that car. The suppliers liked it, but it's over. Face it."

He slammed a fist into her face, then her stomach. She doubled over, grabbed her abdomen. Screamed. Though with the breath knocked out of her, the scream was more like a whisper. She struggled to catch her breath, then suddenly began convulsing, liquid frothed from her mouth. The spasms grew more violent and then she was still, not breathing.

Dammit. He suspected immediately what had happened. What should he do? Try and recover the drugs? He had nothing with which to slice her open, someone might come along and see him in the act. Too risky. He'd have to cut his losses. Make up a story that the mule had not shown up. Promise another girl and delivery right away.

He looked at the nearby creek the local yokels called a river. The water flowed swiftly, running full with the spring rains. He jerked the diamonds from her ears and nose, the sapphire ring. The rock in the navel piercing was gone. It might have come out during her convulstions, no time to look for it. He dragged her slight body over to the bank and threw it out as far as possible. The current took her and she disappeared beneath the fast-moving water.

He went back to the car to get the roll of cash she carried in her purse. He thumbed through the fat roll of bills. It was short. Horny little greaser bitch stole his money. A crumpled piece of paper lay on the floor, almost underneath the seat. He snatched the paper and put it in his pocket. Couldn't risk leaving the dome light on long enough to read it. He returned to the weed-grown creek bank, looked at the purse. Damn thing had cost a lot of money, maybe he could pawn it, recover the money she stole. No, too risky.

After tossing the purse, he went back to the car again. Where to ditch it? He didn't want to leave it near where she'd died. Needed to create as much confusion as possible. With luck they'd think her death was from a normal drug overdose.

He drove along the lane beside the creek to the two lane county road. Turned left. After a couple of miles he came to the condos. Oh, yeah. He turned in and parked in a visitor space for the building next to Harry's. He called Harry's number. God, let him be home.

"What's up, man? We gonna party tonight?"

"Sure thing. But I need you to do something for me first. Come down and take me back to my car."

"Back to your car? How the hell did you get here?"

"Never mind that. Drive around the next building to the visitor parking. I'm in a gold Infiniti."

"Okay. In five."

He used the time to wipe down the car with a handkerchief, just in case, stuck the gloves in his pocket. When Harry drove by he jumped in and said, "Drive."

There was little traffic on the two lane road. He had Harry drop him a hundred yards from the service station and instructed him to drive on into town. They'd meet up again at the Clare View. After Harry left, he started walking. He stepped into the bushes while a couple of cars passed and disappeared. When he reached the station he walked quickly to his car, glad he'd parked on the side. The foreign-born clerk inside wouldn't see him.

He drove away, unaware that being so remote, the station had cameras all around its perimeter.

Five

I had a couple of other cases to clear up before I could spend a lot of time trying to find Mindy's boyfriend. Then when I took my car in for a routine oil change on Thursday afternoon they found a couple of belts so worn they were about ready to break and I had to leave it.

Stuck at home without transportation Friday I determined to do some housekeeping chores I'd been postponing. After several hours of vacuuming, dusting, cleaning bathrooms, I threw in the towel, literally, and decided to switch to sit down work at my desk.

I was slowly becoming used to my new office and home. Both were mine only because my late friend and mentor, Dan Traynor, no longer needed them. Dan had died saving my life. With his last breath, even as I begged him to stay with me, he'd managed to whisper instructions to look for an envelope in his desk.

After his funeral I went to Dan's house with our mutual friend, Detective Shac Lane, and found the handwritten letter in the desk drawer just where he'd said. It turned out he'd done all the legal stuff to turn over his PI business and everything he owned to me before our ill-fated encounter with a murderess. He'd anticipated losing his license because he'd withheld information in the case and was planning to leave town. I hadn't been sure I could bear to live and work here. But Shac convinced me that Dan would be hurt, if that were possible wherever his spirit now resided, if I didn't at least try to accept his gift.

I sank into his desk chair, part of the unwanted legacy. Only God knew how deeply I yearned to be able to change the past and have Dan back in that chair. Even if it meant the bitch who'd killed him would still be alive, too. Never one to dwell on the impossible, I figured I better not start now.

My case expenses needed to be itemized, invoices prepared and mailed this week. Since this was Wednesday and Saturday was the last day of the month an anemic bank account was pushing me. My PI business was not exactly overwhelmed with clients, but I'd let the paperwork I hated from several recent cases accumulate. Which is unfortunate since people tend to want itemized statements when they're paying a chunk of money for expenses incurred on their behalf.

My chair rolled sideways a little and I scooted it back.

First I tackled some real file straightening. In the process I discovered that I was missing my copy of the receipt I'd given Mindy Clark/Goren. Oh well. I did have the signed contract. I clicked on the link for the database website a couple more times. Still unavailable.

I called it quits after an hour or so, closed and locked the file cabinet. I put the other two uncompleted case files, along with Mindy's, in my floor safe. There were still a number of Dan's old case files in the safe. I needed to find the strength to go through and shred them. Another day.

I stood for a moment and stretched. The garage had said my car should be ready by mid-afternoon. About the time I thought about it, I heard the sound of tires in my driveway. I went outside and gave the driver a check along with a tip for bringing my car out. He thanked me and climbed into the garage's car, driven by another employee, and they left. I went back inside, turned out the lights and headed down the hall to the living quarters. Just as I reached the living room the phone rang. The caller ID showed a Georgia number and Juanita Tejoso's name.

"Hello, Juanita. How are things in Georgia?"

"Oh, Cam. Not good. I'm so worried." She sounded distraught, hardly able to talk.

"What, Juanita? Take a deep breath. Tell me what's wrong."

"Please, come. We need your help. Will you come?"

I tried to pry loose some more information about why I should come to Georgia. But she still wouldn't tell me why she, or she and Greg, her husband, had to see me, in person. I agreed to drive down first thing in the morning.

I managed to get a few facts. The trouble had to do with her daughter, Lora. There'd been some trouble a week or so before. Lora hadn't come home on time after spending an afternoon with another girl. Greg found them and brought Lora home. She was okay. But now she was gone again.

"Juanita, call Detective Jake Hunter at the police department. Please, you must."

"No, no, and you mustn't either. Promise me."

"Why? Tell me why not."

Before we hung up, she again insisted, "Cam. You can't tell anyone you're coming. Promise me."

She was so upset, I finally agreed.

Six

The lithe young woman's sandals slapped the paved path that wound through the park on the mountain. She stopped abruptly and stepped off into the spring undergrowth among the trees. She'd spotted something bright, maybe yellow, in the distance. When she approached the spot she saw that it was a patch of yellow roses. Fresh and still dew-laden, several bushes were crowded with the glowing blossoms. A few spent ones lay on the soft ground. She was usually moving too fast to notice nature's splendor and was captivated by their beauty, untended, on top of a mountain. She picked up a fallen blossom and stuck it in her pocket.

Someone coughed nearby, then she heard a voice. "Hey! What are you doing over there in the wilderness?"

She looked around, saw the person she'd been waiting for standing on the path she'd left. "Come on over. Look at these beautiful roses."

He shook his head. "Hell with nature. I'm not going to ruin these five hundred dollar shoes just to breathe in the pollen from some flowers."

The girl laughed and started back toward the path. "Only paved streets for you, huh, city slicker!"

"You're right about that. I've never seen you taking a stroll in the countryside before, either."

She stepped onto the path and into his arms. He kissed her forehead and would have let her go, but she clung to him. "We could take a ride on the barge around the lake. I've heard it's a nice excursion."

"No time. I've got to leave for Atlanta at one o'clock."

"Take me with you. You cancelled our Gatlinburg weekend. I want to be with you."

"I want to be with you, too. But if your mother ever finds out we've been together, she'll kick me out of the firm."

"You're a smart lawyer. You don't need my mother. You could open your own office."

"I told you. I need her connections. And it takes money to open a law office."

The girl crossed her arms and stared at him. "We need to talk. I'm going to Atlanta with you."

"We'll talk about it. Let's go back down to the dam."

She took his arm again and they walked along the paved path back to the parking area. She chattered about what they could do in Atlanta, clubs they could check out, restaurants.

They strolled from the deserted lower parking lot, where he'd left his car, along the short path which led toward the dam. She turned her face up to him, expecting a kiss.

Quick as a viper the man's fist shot out and hit her on the jaw. She had no time to even register surprise at this action by the man she thought was in love with her. She lay on the ground, out cold.

The man pulled a coil of thin but strong rope from his jacket pocket and hurriedly bound her wrists and ankles. He looked around every few seconds to see if anyone was approaching the dam. Hoisting her over his shoulder, he walked as fast as he could back to his car. He clicked his remote to open the trunk and dumped her limp body beside his suitcase. He tore two strips off the roll of gray duct tape he'd put there and slapped them across her mouth.

With a final glance around he slammed the trunk lid with relief. He didn't notice that at least two surveillance cameras, put in place after two murders at the dam the year before, had recorded everything he'd done.

Seven

I'd tried the subscription database on my house computer several times since leaving the office and it was still down so I couldn't renew my membership and access it before leaving town. Who knew if it would be up before Monday, since so many companies had cut out personnel. I gave up for the night and since I had my wheels back, decided to drive to the nearest Subway for some dinner.

I opened my front door and was almost run down by Shac Lane. He plowed straight through my living room and on to my kitchen. During the day he usually came to my office entrance. I don't usually pay much attention to the clock when I'm on a case. How he always knew where I was, office or house, was a mystery I hadn't solved. Dusk had fallen but due to daylight savings time there was still some light in the sky, even though the clock said the time was almost seven o'clock and on Friday last week darkness would have fallen by that time.

"Please. Come in, Shac." I put down my bag and set his usual mug of coffee on the counter in front of him. I always kept a pot going and he knew it. He pulled a photograph from his shirt pocket. It was almost '*déjà vu* all over again,' as Yogi Berra is alleged to have said, when I looked at the picture.

The photo showed a woman, of indeterminate age, lying on the ground. I could see water at the edge of the print. Pond, lake or stream I couldn't tell. Dark hair spread on the ground around her head. Not blonde, as had been the last two female murder victims whose pictures Shac had shown me. The face looked pale and bloated. Dark stockings or tights stretched around swollen legs. No shoes. A torn top revealed a dark lacy bra, but she wore no pants or skirt. Part of a tattoo was just visible on the left shoulder. What appeared to be a scarf seemed to be wound around her neck.

"Strangled? Drowned? Raped?"

"Maybe. Won't know for sure until the autopsy results. Lower clothing may have been pulled off by water action. Recognize her?"

I just looked at him.

"Just an idea. Medical Examiner didn't think she'd been in the water too long. Checking with you in case she came through the battered women's shelter."

"Even if she did, I probably wouldn't recognize her from that picture. But even in it, she looks a little young for the shelter."

"Yeah. I'd go with closer to teen age." He'd seen many more dead bodies than I had, so I couldn't dispute his assessment.

"Who found her and when?" I asked. He might tell me and he might not.

He was looking at the photo and answered in an absent tone. "Hiker. Late yesterday afternoon. Came down off the mountain, walking on the other side of the river and saw her washed up on the bank. Called 911."

"I haven't heard any news of a missing young woman in Wexler Bend."

"None on file. We're widening the inquiry. Could be from Knoxville area or up in Virginia."

"At least she wasn't found at the dam or somewhere on the mountain." I shuddered, pushed away the thought of my own close brush with death after being thrown over the dam. "Did the ME give you a guess as to cause of death?"

"Said she couldn't from a cursory examination. Just didn't think was drowning. Dead maybe a day, could be two. Being in the water, which is cold this time of year, could affect apparent time of death."

"Did the evidence tech get viable fingerprints?"

He rolled his hand. "Iffy. You know what water does to skin."

"Hope it's not a local girl. Though it's sad for any young girl to be murdered. At least, you must think it might be a homicide. Since you're a homicide detective." I refilled his coffee mug and looked up when he didn't answer. He seemed preoccupied again. "What?"

"Nothing. It is sad."

I watched him pick up the photograph in its clear plastic envelope and stuff it in his shirt pocket. I had the feeling he was talking about more than a young woman found dead beside the river. (Note. What was Shac thinking about?)

"I'll order pizza since I didn't make it for my fast food fill-up. Have you eaten?"

Shaking his head, 'no,' he pulled his wallet out and threw a twenty on the counter. I didn't argue, just picked up the phone and ordered two mediums, one cheese and one pepperoni.

"So what are you working on? Runaway husband? Absconding accountant?"

I didn't take offense. Shac knew my first choice had been to join him on the force when I was laid off. My five-member security staff and I all lost our jobs when Eastern Fabricators merged with Southern Moldings. Just my luck, I was just over a year past the Wexler Bend Police Department's minimum age for new hires. Shac had actually gone to the brass and tried to get them to make an exception, given my experience. No dice. So I'd apprenticed to local PI Dan Traynor, one of my Roswell, Georgia classmates, who had relocated to Wexler Bend. After a year I'd passed the Tennessee PI Examination and branched out on my own.

"Runaway boyfriend. Maybe. But I'm driving to Georgia tomorrow."

Shac jerked his head up, eyes narrowed. He didn't say anything for a few seconds, then apparently tried for a casual question. "Going to see Jake?"

I shrugged. "Not specifically. Might call him while I'm down there."

"You've kept in touch with Juanita Tejoso, haven't you? Will you see her?"

"Might see her. It'd be interesting to see how Grandpa's farm looks with houses all over it."

"Won't it be hard, bring back bad memories?"

"I don't think so. Those were the happier years of my childhood. Hopefully it will be for Juanita's kids and those of the other families who bought houses there."

"Her 'kids' aren't exactly kids, are they? Teenagers?"

I didn't want to get into the ages of Juanita's offspring. I tried never to lie to Shac, but I'd promised Juanita not to tell anyone of her call.

"I guess so. But it's still better to finish growing up in the 'burbs than in the metro area." My gut quivered despite my confident words, knowing as I said them, the 'burbs were not always better.

Shac had pulled the dead girl's picture out again. "Wonder where she grew up. Designer scarf and clothing, what she was wearing. ME said the tattoo on her shoulder was not a common one around here. And also not cheap."

"Did she know where it might be more common?"

"Metro areas. Larger cities. We're checking the body art and ink databases."

We kicked around ideas about the girl's possible identity for a while longer. The only new thing he told me was that she'd apparently also worn body jewelry. Several piercings on her ear lobes, one on the side of her nose, and a navel piercing, but no rings or studs were found anywhere near the body. Either her killer kept them for their worth if they were expensive, or was afraid they would reveal who she was too soon. Especially if the jewelry was on par with the clothing. He, or she, had to know that the victim would most likely be identified sooner or later, and wanted to delay it.

Shac left around nine. I took the pizza boxes out and threw them in the outside garbage can. Emptied the dishwasher, wiped the counters, then turned in. I wanted to get an early start for Georgia the next morning.

Eight

Vivian struggled back to consciousness. At first she couldn't remember what had happened. She was lying on a cold surface. She could feel that her feet were bare. Why were they bare? If she'd somehow lost those sandals her stepmother would be furious. She despised her stepmother, but Vivian couldn't refuse the signature red Candy Lorrs covered with brilliant crimson rhinestones when Louise presented them to her as a birthday gift. How had she known? What did it matter now. She needed to get up and find her shoes.

When she tried to move her arms she realized her hands were tied together with something that felt like rope. And when she tried to open her eyes she saw only darkness. Something clothlike covered them and most of her face. Something was stuck to her mouth, it hurt her lips when she tried to speak. Panic tried to enter her mind, but she willed it back. There must be an explanation. Think. Now she remembered. She'd been on the mountain with Marcus. They'd argued because she wanted to go to Atlanta with him. Had something happened to Marcus? Relief flooded her when she heard his voice somewhere above her. Then was canceled by what he said. It made no sense to her.

"Twenty-five thousand. She's worth it. Beautiful. Healthy. White. You'll make the money for that last shipment back in a week."

Derisive laughter in what sounded like two other voices. "Look at the bruises on her arms and legs. We'll have to wait a week for the damage you did to the merchandise to heal before we can even try to market her."

"In a dimly-lit room, who'll see? Look at the shape of those legs. She's perfect. In great shape."

Vivian felt her skirt being lifted. Her skin crawled, but she tried to lie still. A horrible suspicion was dawning in her mind. They were sex-slave traffickers. Marcus was negotiating to sell her into sexual slavery. Forced to endure the most vile acts any human animal with enough money to pay her captors could dream up.

Her mind screamed, 'No.' She'd die first. Since there were at least two others besides Marcus present she knew her chance of escape was slim to nonexistent. But if at all possible she wanted to take Marcus with her. Furious tears threatened, but she fought them back. She'd thought he loved her, wanted to marry her. Had his real game plan all along been to sell her to sexual predators? Please, God, just a tiny opportunity. The next words she heard could be it.

"Let's have a look at her face. You say she's beautiful. But you've probably damaged it, too."

"No. No. She is. I'll take the mask off. Shine the light in her face."

Even through the mask she could tell that a bright light was now shining directly on her head. She had to be ready. She'd slowly inched her legs into position while they argued. God, please let those years of martial arts and running help me do this.

She kept her eyes closed as the mask was stripped over her head. Marcus had sounded as though he was on her left side. She got ready. As soon as the mask was clear, she sprang to her feet, the muscles of her runner's legs propelling her upward. She kept her head lowered slightly, eyes slitted, to avoid looking directly into the light. Through the slits she glimpsed two men jump back. And then she saw Marcus. She charged him. Even bound, her hands were weapons to be reckoned with. She connected with the side of his head, though not where she had hoped. Something, a stick or pole of some kind, was shoved between her legs, tripping her. She glimpsed stacked ranks of concrete blocks just before her head connected with the sharp corner of the top one on the stack.

Nine

Saturday noon

I pulled into the parking lot across from the Roswell Police Headquarters. Jake was waiting out front. I'd asked him to join me at Burger King where he'd suggested we talk the last time I was in Georgia. Juanita was adamant that the police not be involved so I wasn't going to mention her daughter. I'd just try to pick Jake's brain about any recent young women who might have disappeared. I had a gut feeling Juanita was keeping something back, not telling me everything about Lora's disappeance. Why not, I wondered, if she was so desperate for my help? Did she suspect someone the family knew? How did she expect me to help if she didn't level with me?

I pulled to the curb and Jake climbed in the passenger door of my Impreza. "Nice wheels. Good thing you're driving. Brakes went out on my Subaru yesterday."

"Just got this one out of the shop yesterday. Were you moving when they went?"

"Yeh. But I managed to stop. About stripped the gears when I slammed the transmission into neutral and shoved the emergency brake on."

"Sounds like something I'd do." I laughed. I knew detectives even in the Metro Atlanta area didn't pull down the big bucks. And I also knew from painful experience that to replace a transmission cost said big bucks.

"So what brings you to Georgia? Thinking of moving back?"

"God, no."

He placed his hand over his heart and moaned. "I'm hurt. You make it sound as though living in Georgia is akin to dwelling in the nether regions."

I'd never admit it to Jake, but his presence made the remote possibility of moving back to Georgia a tiny fraction more palatable to me. I felt disloyal to Shac even thinking the thought. But after all, Shac had never made any actual moves to make me believe he even considered the possibility we might become a 'couple,' as in real dating. True, he'd been injured after he planned to sleep on my couch, as a bodyguard, when an unknown person was threatening me. But he never followed up, so we remained just friends.

Jake had come back into my life during the time we worked on a case last year involving my ex-husband and his biological father. We kept in touch via email and the occasional phone call. I got the impression he was waiting to see what my relationship with Shac turned out to be. So was I.

I spotted the Burger King sign ahead and pulled into the entrance. We went in.

"You're buying, I hope?" Jake said. "Had to give the brake place a down payment with my last few dollars."

"Sure. Since it was my idea. Put my repairs on plastic." I laughed. "Maybe you should change professions."

"Maybe I will, one day." He put his arm around my shoulder and squeezed. "I'm glad to see you again, Cam."

A tingle rippled through me and I almost leaned into him. But that nagging sense of disloyalty to Shac stopped me.

We walked to the counter and gave our orders to the bored counter clerk. When our food came we took our tray to a table near the back of the dining area and busied ourselves with smothering fries in ketchup.

Jake took a bite of double-cheese Whopper and chewed, closing his eyes in gustatory delight. The man did like his Burger King sandwiches. After he swallowed, he opened his eyes and looked at me. "So. Why?"

I had been going over all the possible reasons I could give him for being back in Roswell. I decided to stay close to the truth. It's easier than trying to remember what lie you told. I'd done plenty of lying in my work as a private investigator.

But lying to someone you were pretty sure was up to no good and lying to a friend are two different things.

"Wanted to get away for a few days. Thought I'd visit Juanita, see what all the developers did to my grandparents old farm."

"Don't think it'll be too sad?"

"it will be sad. But I'm a big girl, now. I can deal with a little nostalgia."

"I'm sure you can. The Senator left Juanita a lot of money, didn't he?"

"Yes. Most of it in trust for her children. But enough to her so they could pay off their mini-farm. Greg was able to start up his small business,.portrait photography. Seems to be doing okay with it."

"Sad case, that. The senator's wife murdering both his biological children." He slapped his forehead. "Hell. I'm sorry, Cam. One of them was your ex."

"Forget it. Sometimes an abuser gets what he deserves. Maybe I shouldn't feel like that, but it's the truth."

" He put you through enough. Can't say I disagree. And you can't deny how you feel."

I looked into his eyes. They held such an intense expression I wondered if he might have been referring to more than my lack of compassion for my ex. Mentally I shook my head. Must stop thinking about what Jake might be feeling. I'd begin to despise myself for being less than forthcoming about my presence in Georgia.

"So. Working on any interesting cases?" I asked, to change the subject.

"Define interesting." He threw the ball back into my court.

I shrugged. "Murder. Conspiracy. Big drug case. Though I guess the Task Force I saw on the news works those. Wait a minute. You're on the Task Force."

It was his turn to shrug. "You know the metro area. Always something going on. More white collar crime, too, with the economy. Local bank president was just indicted for embezzling a few million dollars. Some poor schmuck uses a nine mil to rob a convenience store of a few hundred. Guess who'll serve time, the bank exec or the schmuck."

"I caught a mention on the car radio about a young woman found dead behind a convenience store here. Was it a robbery gone bad? Or something else?"

Did I imagine his look sharpened? "Maybe. Just thrown out beside the dumpster. Can't find anyone who knew her."

I hoped my own expression still showed just normal interest. His case sounded a lot like the one Shac had caught. The young woman, unknown in Wexler Bend, found dead beside the river. But surely there couldn't be a connection between the cases of two young murdered women three hundred miles apart. Right. And who would have thought there'd be a connection between a party girl murdered thirty years ago in a mass shooting in an Atlanta hotel and a beautiful hotel bartender in Wexler Bend?

I decided to throw down a card. "Shac's caught a bad one at home. Young woman found dead beside the river, no ID yet."

Jake took another bite of his sandwich. People not involved in law enforcement wonder how cops and detectives can eat and still talk about appalling subjects. It's simple. They have to eat to live. Their jobs routinely expose them to unspeakable horrors so they'd starve if they couldn't eat.

"Drowned?" He asked, dragging a French fry through ketchup.

"Maybe. He hadn't told me when I left."

"No locals unaccounted for?"

"No, so he said."

We continued talking various past cases in general terms. I appreciated that Jake treated me as an equal, as Shac did. Even though in actual fact, we were far from it. And their bosses were not above pointing it out. I barely knew Jake's boss, Lieutenant Patrice Consolo. Jake seemed to get along with and respect her. Shac's boss, Chief of Detectives Captain DeWitt Tawson was a hardass, but a straight shooter. I respected him. I was sure Shac did, too, though with Shac, it's hard to tell.

Jake's cell phone rang. He wiped his mouth and answered. "Hey?" He listened for a moment. I thought he was avoiding eye contact. I chalked it up to imagination and tried to look like I wasn't interested in his conversation. He said a few noncommital words. Then, "I'll be in the office in half an hour or so. See you then." He ended the call and stuck his phone back in his shirt pocket.

"Sorry. Where were we?"

"You probably need to get to work. And I need to head on to Canna Lily Farms. I'd like to get back to Wexler Bend before dark."

We gathered up our wrappers and cups and Jake dumped them in the trash receptacle. I drove him back to Headquarters and dropped him off. His attention seemed to be divided between me and whatever his phone call had been about.

"Later, Cam." He waved and went through the big double doors.

Ten

As I turned off Cobb Parkway toward Canna Lily Farms, my own cell phone rang. I pulled into an empty driveway to an abandoned business with broken windows and looked at the screen. Juanita.

"Juanita. What's happened?"

"Lora is home, Cam. She is okay. You don't need to come here after all."

Like hell. "I'm almost there, Juanita. I'll see you in a few minutes." I hung up before she could protest more.

I hadn't driven all this way not to talk to her. Not with the suspicions I harbored about the nature of her Lora's disappearance. And now the mystery of her reappearance.

The stone pillars at the entrance of Canna Lily Farms subdivision were taller than they'd looked in the online pictures I'd looked at. I drove between the pillars, the pair of wrought iron gates were for ornamentation only apparently. In an open position they seemed to be permanently embedded in the professionally landscaped grounds around the entrance. The main features of the landscaping were huge beds of scarlet Canna lilies. It was like looking at Grandma's signature flower-filled beds all around her farmhouse.

Tears stung the corners of my eyes and I angrily brushed them away. Long past time for tears. Grandma and Grandpa were gone, resting in the cemetery two miles away. I'd go later to pay my respects and place red lilies on their graves. I hadn't had time when I was here last year. Remembering that trip, it still seemed so unlikely I would soon meet a cousin of my ex-husband's sister, who even then lived on the site of my grandparent's farm. Where my mother and I lived with them for several years. The happiest years I'd enjoyed when I was growing up.

The same old unanswerable questions tried to push into my mind. Why had my mother married my abusive, and worse, stepfather? Why hadn't she left him sooner? Maybe he wouldn't have killed her, as I was sure he had. Though he'd never been charged with the murder.

I shoved those thoughts back in the deep place where I tried to keep them. They rarely escaped unless I was in Georgia, where it had all taken place.

I spotted the blue mailbox surrounded by more tall, red Canna lilies. My destination. I hoped I could pull more information from Juanita when we talked face-to-face. On the phone I'd pulled the bare fact from her that it had to do with Lora not coming home one night a week or so ago. Her father had gone out searching at the hangouts she and her friends frequented. He'd tracked her and another girl to a local motel. They told him they'd been accosted when they left the cafe where they'd met a classmate. Some men had forced them into a van, took them to the motel and threatened their families if the girls left. He brought Lora home, but the other girl refused to leave.

"And you didn't call the police, Juanita?" I'd practically screamed.

"Greg wouldn't let me." Juanita said, sobbing. "He's hardly allowed Lora outside after he brought her home. She threatened to run away and now maybe she has. You have to help us, Cam."

So here I was, back in Georgia, about to get embroiled in yet another probably heart-breaking case. I hated to deceive Juanita. I'd known I needed to talk to Jake before seeing her. I'd looked up the archived *Atlanta Journal-Constitution* recent newspaper articles about missing girls. There were several. I knew by the carefully worded police reports that human traffickers were suspected. I'd jumped to the same conclusion myself when Juanita told me what the girls had said after Greg found them at the motel.

Of course, Jake had not alluded to the possibility when I tried to worm it out of him back at Burger King. I was pretty sure he'd suspected I was after some particular information and deliberately hadn't told me as much as he could have.

He'd quickly covered his reaction when I mentioned hearing on the news about the murdered girl found behind the convenience store so I knew there was more. He was on the Joint Drug and Human Trafficking Task Force so his expression, before he covered it, had reinforced my guess that one or both of those crimes was involved in the girl's death.

I turned in beside the mailbox and continued down the curved driveway which ended in front of double garage doors. Time to get some answers from Juanita and Greg after her frantic second call late last night. Lora was gone again. She hadn't left a note so they didn't know if, tired of Greg's tight rein, she had made good her threat to run away again.

Juanita's eyes were red and swollen when she let me in. She hugged me.

"You should have called, Cam. It would have saved you the drive. Lora is back home again." She seemed nervous and kept glancing toward the door I was pretty sure led to the kitchen/dining area. "Greg is back in his dark room. I'll get him."

"Wait, Juanita." But she hurried away. I'd wanted to talk to her a few minutes without Greg being present. I thought I might get more information.

She held onto his arm when they returned. His face, too, looked as though he'd been through hell. As might be expected. I didn't have a daughter, but I could imagine how terror would strike a parent's heart when a child could not be found. Imagination would paint the worst scenario. The pictures from last year and the one I'd recently seen of girls for whom the truth of such a tragedy had been true flashed through my mind. I mentally shook it away. At least Lora was home, safe. Wasn't she?

We sat in the cozy family room, though I could tell they wished I had not come. Maybe they thought if they denied anything was wrong, it wouldn't be. A mindset I was well acquainted with, too.

"Did she tell you where she went?" I asked.

41

"She wouldn't, at first. Finally she said she went back to the motel to find her friend. But she wasn't there."

"Do you think the girl went back home? Did Lora say who she was?"

Greg kept twisting his hands, popping his knuckles. "We don't know. Lora won't give her name."

"She turns to the wall, won't talk." Juanita buried her head on Greg's shoulder. "She says she won't talk to the police, not even you. We told her you're not police. That maybe you can help. She says no one can." The distraught mother looked up, unvarnished terror in her eyes.

"I'm so sorry, Juanita. I'll do anything I can. Let me try and talk to her."

But it was no use. Lora wouldn't look at me. Wouldn't answer any of my questions. I finally patted her shoulder. Told her I'd be there any time she wanted to talk.

"What good is money, if you can't keep your child safe?" Juanita cried when we returned to the living room. "I wish my cousin, Gloria, never found out who she was. I wish the senator never left us the money, that we were back in the city."

Greg patted her, held her. "Thanks for coming, Cam. If we learn anything else and think you can help, we'll call."

"Please do."

He kissed Juanita's cheek, said, "I'll see Cam out. I'll be right back."

She nodded.

I walked over and hugged her. "You'll get through this. I know it."

Greg plodded heavily beside me to my car. "I think I agree with my wife. We were doing all right. I'd rather work for someone else and my family be safe."

I tried to phrase a question so it wouldn't upset him even more. "Why do you think the girls were taken? Was it money? Ransom?"

"No one called and demanded money. Besides we don't have that much money." He looked at me with haunted eyes. "I haven't told Juanita. But I've heard stories. About girls kidnapped and taken away. Forced to do – things."

"I wondered if you knew anything about that possibility."

"The first time, when I found her at the motel, she and the other girl said the men threatened their families. That's why she won't talk, I'm sure. Would they? Hurt the girls' families?"

What to say to him? We both knew it would be an effective threat used to keep young girls in line. "I don't know for sure. But the girls, women, too, believe them. The Federal government, Georgia, Tennessee, some other states, have formed a task force to try and stop this wicked crime."

"How I pray they can."

"So do I, Greg. So do I."

I got into my car, my own heart heavy with their pain.

I wanted to return to Wexler Bend and get back to work on my missing boyfriend case. Against my better judgment I decided to drive back to the Roswell Police Station and tell Jake goodbye. Of course, there was no personal reason. He was just a good friend. He'd been called out to a crime scene before we'd finished our Burger King meal earlier.

Eleven

I reached for the handle of the police station's big double doors just as they pushed outward, almost knocking me to the sidewalk.

"Hey, watch where you're going, will you?" I said, holding on to the handle for balance.

"Sorry, sorry." A familiar voice spoke. "Cam? You must have got a real early start. I tried to call you before I left. Why aren't you back home by now?"

"And why are you in Georgia? You didn't mention you were coming, too. This is a long way to come to keep an eye on me."

He barked a short laugh. "You don't really think Tawson would authorize a road trip to Roswell, Georgia just to keep an eye on you?"

"No, now that I think of it. So why are you here?"

"Ask your boyfriend."

"My what? Jake? Don't be ridiculous." Don't let him sidetrack you, I scolded myself.

"I told you why I was coming to Georgia. To see a friend." Well, that's all it turned out to be. I hadn't really lied. Had I? "What about you?"

"Ask him." Shac Lane only gave out information when it suited him. Of course, as a detective on the Wexler Bend police force, he did have constraints I didn't as a PI. He'd barreled out of the Roswell Police Station as if on an important mission, but he made no move to leave, still holding the doors open. So I decided to push a little more.

"Does this trip have anything to do with the girl found by the river?"

Jake walked up behind Shac. "The girl you told me about, Cam?"

"I thought she might recognize her. If she'd come through the women's shelter, maybe." Shac answered.

Jake's eyes narrowed. "Why'd you think she might have come from the shelter?"

"Just a thought, no stone, et cetera." Shac looked a question at Jake.

"Shac, do you have to leave right now?" Jake looked back.

"I can stay a little longer. Why?"

"I'd like to talk to both of you for a few minutes," Jake replied.

I shrugged and followed them inside. I was thinking as hard as I could, trying to come up with a plausible reason for being in Roswell without breaking my promise to Juanita. I was pretty sure Shac didn't buy the idea I'd just come down to visit Juanita and put flowers on my grandparents' graves. In point of fact I had the bouquets in my car, though I hadn't made it to the cemetery. He knew Juanita and Greg's house sat on part of the land which had been my grandparents' farm. He would put two and two together sooner rather than later if Lora's abduction came to light.

We didn't talk as we passed through the detective squad room. I nodded to a couple of the men I'd met when I was there last year. Jake took us back to the small conference room next to one of their interrogation rooms. I silently thanked him. Interrogation rooms were not on my list of favorite places to be. What could he want to talk to me about that included Shac? I guessed I'd find out in a few minutes.

Jake opened the door, entered and took a seat at the end of the well-worn wood table that took up most of the room. He indicated the coffee pot on a utility stand along one wall, but we both declined. Police station coffee is palatable only if nothing else is available.

Only then did I notice someone else was already seated at the table. TBI Special Agent Taylor Glass was as impeccably dressed as always, in a well-pressed blue business suit, hair and makeup perfect. I think if the woman was in the middle of ninety-mile an hour hurricane winds, not a hair would be out of place. She acknowledged us with a nod and a half-smile in my direction. I assumed she had seen Shac already. I returned her nod.

"Well, Tennessee seems well-represented in the room, Jake. What's going on?" I am not one to stand on protocol. I hadn't been ordered here so I felt I had a right to be dealt in on this game, whatever it was.

Jake said, "I'm guessing you both know Taylor is a member of a new Multi-State Task Force which includes Tennessee, Georgia, Alabama, and several other southeastern states?"

"I saw a news clip before I left home. Congratulations, Taylor," I replied.

She nodded again.

"So why are just the two of you here? Where are the other members from Georgia who I saw were also on the Task Force?"

"I'll get to that. But I need you two to swear not to reveal anything you hear in this room. When we need to release something to the public, we'll do another press conference." Jake's voice had a stern note I'd not heard before. If not for the nature of the crime his task force was investigating I'd have gotten up and left in a huff. I suspected Shac was having some of the same thoughts. And I also suspected Jake knew it.

"You're professionals. But I had to say it for the record. Now, Cam, I know why Shac is here. Can you tell me honestly, to the best of your knowledge, that whatever brought you to Roswell has no connection, none whatever, to the crime, or crimes, the Task Force is working on?"

No doubt he correctly interpreted the expression I couldn't keep from my face for the hard, un-Jake-like note returned to his voice with his next words. "I can convene a formal meeting of more of the Task Force members and compel you to answer, Cam."

"And if I refuse?" I could be stubborn, too.

"Cam. Don't. You know better." Shac put a hand on my arm. I shook it off.

"A subpoena, of course. And arrest if you refuse to comply. You do know that, Ms. Locke."

I slumped in my chair, resistance temporarily gone. Never before had Jake called me 'Ms. Locke.' This was dead serious.

"A friend called, asked me to look into something to do with her daughter."

Jake said nothing. Waited.

"Her daughter didn't come home one night after going out with friends. Her husband went looking for her and found their daughter and one of the friends at a motel. He brought her home. The other girl stayed."

Jake still waited.

"My friend was hysterical, distraught because her daughter had disappeared again. She wanted me to come down and look for her, but made me promise not to tell anyone she'd called me. I urged her to go to the police, but she said she was afraid to do that."

"Why?"

"The girls were told their families would be killed if they didn't stay at the motel, so the other girl wouldn't leave. Juan — my friend, thought her daughter may have gone to try and help the other girl and fallen into their hands again."

Jake looked up from his notes. "The friend who called is Juanita Tejoso?"

I nodded.

"Her daughter is still missing?"

"No. She had arrived home just before I got to the Tejoso house. She wouldn't tell them anything, or me when I tried, just lay in bed, turned to the wall, and said she wanted to be left alone."

"The parents take her to a doctor?"

"She said she'd run away again if they made her go. They were afraid to push it."

Jake and Taylor exchanged a glance. Everyone in the room, including me, knew girls and women who were sexually assaulted often refused to tell anyone. You can't force a victim to say anything. They shut down. As Lora was doing. Surely the Task Force wouldn't try to compel her to talk to them. Even if any information she might have about her abductors was crucial to their investigation.

After a few more questions Jake told Shac and me we could go. Shac, the traitor, tried to talk Jake into letting him stay, but Jake was adamant. He walked with us to the door of the station, probably to make sure we left.

Shac and I stood on the sidewalk and stared at the closed doors for a few seconds. "Well, guess we got our walking papers, Cam."

"If they talk to Juanita and Greg, she's going to hate me."

"No 'if' about it, they'll have to talk to them. But they know they won't get anything from the girl if they try to force her to talk. Maybe the Dad can give them something useful."

"I hope. He'll be angry I talked to the police."

"Maybe not. He's probably going along with Juanita, but a man knows he needs help when something like what happened happens." He amended his statement, "Most men."

I changed the subject. "Have you found out anything else about the girl by the river? Identity?"

"Not yet. Tawson released the picture at noon today. The tatt on her shoulder is the work of a woman who only works the Southeastern states. Was employed in a shop in Atlanta until she was charged with tattooing several minors without parental permission."

"You're here to find her? Have you? Talked to her?"

He hesitated, then caught himself. "Moved on to Alabama. That's my next stop."

"Where in Alabama?"

"Place called New Corners."

I was glad my head was down as I searched my purse for my car keys. What was going on? Why did two unrelated cases in Wexler Bend, Tennessee - a girl looking for her supposed boyfriend who'd run out on her and a murdered girl found beside the river - lead back to the same Alabama town? And why had Shac hesitated before answering my questions? Which one didn't he want to answer?

"Found 'em." I held up my keys. "I was afraid I'd have to hitch a ride back home with you."

Shac put on an offended look. "And what would be so horrible about that, may I ask?"

"The horrible part would be riding in the sorry excuse for a police cruiser Kia you drive. And having to bail my Impreza out of impound."

"Rub it in, why don't you? If you'd gotten your wish and become a cop, you too could drive a Kia." But he took my hand and we walked across the street to the parking garage. I have to admit I didn't mind the warm feel of my hand in his. He kissed the top of my head as he opened my car door and I got in. "Be careful. See you back in Tennessee."

I sat for several seconds holding my ignition key and watched him walk away before I came out of my trance. Was I actually swooning over a casual buss from Shac Lane? Not even a first. Had he actually kissed my hair? Had my seeing Jake again been the reason? Or maybe his unexpected handholding and kiss were an attempt to defuse my irritated feelings and keep me out of trouble. Something he seemed to feel he needed to do on a regular basis. He saw my reaction to Jake's insistence on my telling him about Lora's kidnapping in spite of my promise to Juanita. And even though he himself had acted in exactly the same manner toward me in times past.

He only wanted the best for me. And he knew I knew it. Being a man, he probably didn't automatically assume the same for Jake. Shac's character was the definition of integrity. He would never try to insinuate himself between me and someone he thought I cared about. So maybe he thought Jake had overstepped and was no longer a rival. If he'd ever thought he was. Or cared. Which was not a given. Maybe a product of my overactive imagination and I should give it an overhaul.

Twelve

I drove out of the parking structure and onto the street without seeing Shac's Kia. He'd be heading west to Alabama to check out the tattoo artist. I wound around to Cobb Parkway and headed north in the late model Impreza Dan had left me along with his home and business. He'd been from Roswell, too, my date for our high school prom. He'd teased me about the worn-out wreck I drove during the year I apprenticed with him. When I began making a little money working on my own, he persuaded me to buy the Toyota Corolla I sold after I'd finally forced myself to drive the one he left me. I'd miss him and his wry sense of humor forever. When someone sacrifices their life for you, there's no way to repay it. Except to do as much good for others during the life you were given as you possibly can. I hoped that's what I was doing.

When I reached Cartersville I briefly debated taking U.S. Route 411, the more scenic two-lane highway, rather than Interstate 75 through Chattanooga. But I needed to get back to Wexler Bend and close my disappearing boyfriend case. I was a little surprised Mindy Clark, or as I now knew, Mindy Goren, if Mindy was her first name, had not been calling to see what I'd found out about her Whitt. If Whitt was really his first name.

Most of my trip back home was uneventful. But I had a heart-stopping few minutes as I was leaving Chattanooga, headed for Knoxville, on the six-and eight-lane stretch after the I-24 and I-75 split. I always drove in the left hand through lanes on this part of I-75 to avoid idiots careening onto the Interstate from the many on-ramps. On my right a nondescript pickup with dark-tinted windows kept inching over into my lane. I grudgingly gave way, losing speed as much as as I could due to traffic behind me, and then the truck suddenly swerved completely into my lane and slowed.

I had nowhere to go. An oncoming eighteen wheeler was headed straight for my left front bumper. And no time to even glance at my rear view mirror. I stomped my brake pedal as hard as possible. I glimpsed the horror on the trucker's face as he whizzed by with only inches between us. My own and dozens of speeding cars and trucks behind me filled the air with the smell of burning rubber.

In an instant my lane and the three other lanes were filled with vehicles turned in every direction. Some had fishtailed and spun until they were headed almost opposite to the way they'd originally been going. The road was covered in black skid marks, but by some miracle there were no collisions. I tried to spot the pick-up truck which had caused the whole thing, but it had apparently sped off. Since no vehicles had been damaged and traffic had already backed up for at least half a mile, drivers simply shook heads, extricated themselves and left the scene.

Three and a half hours later I pulled into my driveway. And a pair of headlights immediately followed, a Wexler Bend police squad car. I got out of my car and stood waiting as Detective Don Mears walked toward me.

"Cam. Would you come down to the station with me, please?" He tried for business-like, but I could tell he was a little uncomfortable with the request.

"I guess so. What's it about?" I asked.

"I really can't say. Captain Tawson will explain when we get to the station."

"Tawson." I shrugged. "All right. Let me get my purse."

"Hand it to me, please." Mears said firmly.

My face must have shown my shock.

"I assume your gun is in it, right?"

"Of course. You know I'm licensed to carry."

"I'll have to hold it for now." He wasn't backing down, even though he was Shac's partner and we were friends.

I handed over my purse, or tote bag, which I carry instead of a normal pocketbook. He held it under his arm and waited. Without another word I closed my car door and marched to the rear door of the cruiser.

"Get in the front, Cam," he said.

"If I'm going to be treated like a criminal, I'll ride like one." My anger was about to spill over and I hated it but couldn't seem to stop myself.

"In front. Think I want to be anywhere near Shac Lane after I've made you ride in the back of my cruiser?" The corner of his mouth turned up ever so little.

Slightly mollified, I climbed in the front seat. But I still didn't speak to him all the way to police headquarters. Don walked me back to Tawson's office instead of an interrogation room, so I deduced I wasn't about to be charged with a crime.

Chief of Detectives Tawson rose from his desk chair when I entered, which he doesn't normally do. He indicated I should sit in the chair in front of his desk and sat back down when I did. I was beginning to feel little prickles of alarm, remembering my own close call in Chattanooga. Had something happened to Shac?

He waved Don to a second chair. "I'm sorry to have Don bring you in as soon as you got back, Cam. Shac told me approximately when you'd arrive."

Relief went through me and I was glad I was sitting. Shac was all right. "So why am I here, Captain Tawson?" I asked.

"You're aware the body of a young woman was found beside Clare Creek Friday evening?"

"Yes, sir." I said.

"We've identified her. And found her car."

I waited. What did the unfortunate young woman have to do with me? What about her caused Tawson to have Mears drag me down to Police Headquarters?

"We found a receipt for a $200 retainer, with your name as the the payee, in her car. From whom have you received $200 recently?"

Tawson was Shac's superior, but I was getting a little weary today of being treated as though I had no rights. I hadn't done anything wrong, so why was this demand for information a one-way street?

"I'll answer any of your questions I'm legally required to answer. But unless a crime is involved of which I'm aware, you and I both know I'm not obligated to answer."

Tawson rocked back in his chair. Given his bearing and size, as well as position, not many people dared challenge him. But he'd caught me at a bad time. I might regret my belligerence, especially if he took it out on Shac, but I'm stubborn since escaping the clutches of my ex, Emory Locke. Tawson knew my history and he was no fool, probably knew I wasn't just refusing to cooperate on general principles.

"Let's start over. Do you know the name of the person to whom you gave a receipt for two hundred dollars two days ago?" He hesitated a moment. "A receipt found in a murdered woman's car."

"I know the name she gave me. It's the one I wrote on the receipt, Mindy Clark."

"A careful way to put it. Do you believe it was her correct name?" He had me there. I hadn't believed her, but hadn't challenged her on it.

"No. I don't."

"Did you ask for her correct, legal name?"

"No. I don't normally accuse potential clients of lying. Until I find out for sure they are."

"And did you? Find out she was not being truthful about her name?"

"Not definitively. I learned something later and my belief was reinforced that it was not her real name."

Tawson looked at me and sighed. "I really wish you'd just tell me what you know about the young woman who told you her name was Mindy Clark."

"I'm sure there's an important reason you're asking me these questions. At least I hope so. Okay. She called me on Wednesday and made an appointment to come in at two-thirty. I was on my way out to do some errands when she called and she was already parked at my house when I returned. She said she wanted me to find her boyfriend, who had disappeared. At least he wasn't answering her calls or returning them. She said they'd planned to spend the weekend in Gatlinburg so she was worried."

"I'll get back to her visit. Describe her, please."

"Small stature, slender, exquisite make up, dark eyes. Expensive clothes and bling. The dead girl had dark hair, didn't she? This girl was blonde." I waited a beat. "But the hair was a wig, a very good one."

If I expected a reaction from Tawson, it wasn't forthcoming. He said nothing except, "Go on."

"I wasn't to tell him she was looking for him, just let her know he was okay."

"Do you think the person she wanted you to find was her boyfriend?"

I hesitated. "I had my doubts, since she'd lied, I was pretty sure, about her name. But since she didn't want to know where he was, and I spelled that out in the contract she signed, I took her case. But I actually spent most of the little time I've been on the case trying to find out her real name."

"I'll need the contract. Even though I assume she signed with the fake name."

"She did. And I assumed you would. Now will you tell me what connection there is between this girl and the dead girl beside the creek?"

Without answering my question he asked another of his own. "What kind of car did your client drive?"

"Brand new Infiniti, gold, custom wheels. Was she killed in it?" I threw out the question, not expecting an answer.

"She wasn't purposely murdered, in the usual sense," Tawson said, after a few seconds of silence.

I stared at him. "In what sense, then?"

"She was a drug mule." His black eyes bored a hole in me. "If you leak this, your PI and carry license are history, Cam."

I hardly heard his threat. I knew I wasn't about to leak any information. My mind was racing over all his verbal bombshell implied. The daughter of a highly-placed executive at Southern Moldings. A drug mule. Was her father involved? Who else? And who was her supposed boyfriend?

He'd waited for me to absorb the implications. He answered the question I was about to ask. "A balloon of heroin burst in her stomach. From a blow, the ME thinks. Bruised tissue shows up underneath the skin on her abdomen, even though water action obliterated the surface bruising."

I was remembering the chic young woman, who hadn't wanted her 'boyfriend' to know she was looking for him. Was he the one who struck her, causing her death?

"She had diamond studs in her ears, side of her nose." I hardly knew I spoke aloud. "Big ones. And an exquisite sapphire ring."

Tawson waited.

"I guess she had the drugs in her when she was in my office, didn't she?" A cold chill traced down my back. I crossed my arms against my own abdomen and squeezed.

"Yes." He said. "You said you acquired possible information as to her real identity. Who do you think she was?"

"I believe her father is a Vice President at Southern Moldings. Name is Robert Goren. It's mostly conjecture. Do I have to tell you how I came to that conclusion?"

He waved it away. "We know it's correct. Selena Goren. I've talked to her parents. They're shattered. Or so it seems."

I tried to hide my relief. I'd hate myself if I was in any way responsible for bringing trouble down on Maxie.

Tawson got up and came around his desk. "Thank you for your cooperation, Cam. Don will take you home now. We'll call you if we need any other information. But please call if you remember anything else. Will you give Don the contract?"

"Of course. Find out who killed that beautiful girl, even if he didn't intend it."

"We will." Tawson's tone was grim.

When we got to my house I entered through my office and Don came in with me. I gave him the original contract the girl who called herself Mindy had signed and he gave me a receipt for it. I'd already scanned the contract into my computer, of course, though I didn't mention it.

At the door he looked down at me. "Still mad at me?"

"Certainly not, Don. You were doing your job." I felt magnanimous since he'd returned my tote bag as soon as we left the station. I grinned. "And I won't tell Shac you took my bag and held it."

"I appreciate it." He opened the door and stepped across the threshold.

"Don." Something had occurred to me.

"Yeah?" He looked back.

"When I saw Shac in Georgia earlier today, he seemed to have something on his mind. Why was he there, anyway? Besides trying to find the ink slinger."

Don's face fell. "Ah, Cam. Don't ask me. He actually was looking for the tattooist though."

"I'm sure. But there was something else, wasn't there?"

"He'll tell you." Don was a good partner for Shac. I was certain he adhered to the same strict personal code as Shac. I wasn't about to try to undermine their trust in each other.

I smiled. "It's okay. I'll wait till he does."

He looked relieved, sketched a salute and went out. "Good night, Cam."

Thirteen

If I thought my day was done after Mears left I was soon disabused of the notion. I'd gone from my office to my house proper and barely turned toward the kitchen, intending to fix a cup of chamomile tea, when my doorbell pealed the first notes of Elvis Presley's *Hound Dog*. I had to get that tune changed. Dan had been the definitive Elvis fan. I liked the King well enough, but *Hound Dog* was not my favorite of his songs. I briefly considered what I might change it to in the time it took me to reach the front door.

When I opened the door I faced someone I had not seen since leaving Eastern Fabricators. Nate Taggert, the Eastern Vice President who couldn't hold his liquor or keep his hands to himself, stood on my doorstep.

While I stared at him, too surprised to even wonder why he was there, he asked, "May I come in, Cam?"

"Oh, oh, yes. Of course, Mr. Taggert."

I stepped back.

"Nathan. I'm not a high-powered executive lording it over a lowly security chief now. I hope you'll forgive me."

"Twelve Step?" I asked.

His smile was rueful. "Yes. But I've wanted to ask it anyway."

I said, "Okay. What can I do for you? Nathan."

Instead of answering, his next words harked back again to our days at Eastern Fabricators. "Truth be told, I never was this high-powered executive. My father was Chairman of the Board."

"I know," I replied, not able to think of anything else to say.

"I was a VP only because he wanted me to be. No decision-making authority at all. Maybe that's why I drank so much." He hastened to add, "Which is no excuse."

"Are you in need of my professional services, Nathan?" I tried to get back to the reason he was standing in my living room.

"I think I might. If you'd consider taking me on as a client."

"Then why don't we go to my office."

I led the way down the side hall to the inside door to Dan's, now my, office.

He looked around when we entered. "I've never been inside a private detective's office," he remarked. "Nice aquarium. No fish?"

He was probably making conversation to cover unease. I told him the aquarium had belonged to my predecessor, without going into details. Waved him to the client chair at the side of my desk. I pulled a note pad toward me and wrote the date and time. Made a few doodles on the side of the page.

When we were seated I repeated the question I'd asked earlier. "Now what can I do for you?"

"I need to know if my daughter is all right. Her name is Vivian, you may remember."

I nodded automatically, but my pen stopped moving in the middle of drawing my version of a rose blossom on a short stem. His words eerily echoed those of Selena Goren, who had sat in the same chair, was it only a little more than seventy-two hours ago?

"Do you have some reason to think she isn't all right?"

"I've been trying to call her all evening. My calls go straight to voice mail. She always answers since I'm out of rehab."

"When did you last talk to her?"

"Day before yesterday. Her birthday. She told me she might be going to Gatlinburg for a couple of days. But she'd still have service on her phone there."

"Did she mention visiting a friend out of town? Maybe to your ex-wife?"

He looked down at his clasped hands. "I haven't spoken to Louise for a few days. It's better if we don't have too much to do with each other."

I could believe that. Neither did I care to have interaction with Louise Taggert, who was Shac Lane's ex-wife before she married Taggert. And the feeling was very mutual.

Nathan looked up. "She told me not to mention her trip to Louise if I talked to her."

"Oh."

"And there's something else."

He didn't seem to relish telling whatever the 'something else' was. I waited. As Dan had taught me to do.

"I think she has a boyfriend she doesn't want her, Louise, to know about."

"Do you," I put a slight emphasis on the 'you,'."know who the boyfriend is?"

He waited so long to answer I was about to prod him a little. "I think he is the partner in Louise's law firm."

I wrote a few words on the pad, just to have something to do while I digested his idea about the identity of Vivian's boyfriend. I knew Louise's law partner, Marcus Oliver, by reputation only. The son of a judge at the state capital, not known for his impartial rulings, now being mentioned as a possible appointee to the Supreme Court of Tennessee. Rumor had it the fruit didn't fall far from the legal apple tree. The son had been wild as a young man and only missed jail time because of his father.

Louise dumped Shac and married Nathan Taggert just before the sudden merger of Eastern Fabricators and Southern Moldings, when he lost his job. They moved to the Nashville area, then she divorced Taggert and they both moved back to Wexler Bend. Louise brought Marcus Oliver with her. They'd opened a law practice which had quickly flourished, most likely due to their combined connections.

"Why do you think Oliver is her boyfriend?"

"I picked up her phone by accident once when she was visiting my apartment. I noticed several texts from him. I figured he might have been trying to reach Louise. But Vivian snatched it from me and ordered me to leave her phone alone."

"Do you know if Oliver is in town now?"

"I can't be sure. The receptionist wouldn't say when I called the office. I tried to disguise my voice, but I think she recognized it. She worked for Louise before."

"Does Vivian live with Louise?"

"No. I've been by her condo, but she doesn't answer the doorbell."

I tapped my pen against the pad. Did I really want to get involved in this Taggert family affair? But I'd known Taggert, even if I hadn't liked him much, before he married Louise. And a job is a job. A professional takes what jobs present themselves, if it's legal and aboveboard. More of Dan's training whispered in my head.

"All right, Nathan. I'll see what I can find out. I'll need Vivian's vitals, address and phone number, names of friends, anything you can tell me that might help locate her."

He gave me a look of deep gratitude and pulled out his wallet. "Retainer?"

"Remember, Vivian is of age. If I locate her and she doesn't want to be found, I can't divulge her whereabouts."

"I understand. I just don't think that's the case, Cam."

After he gave me the details I needed, a $200 retainer and signed a contract, he became somewhat chatty. From relief maybe.

"My father left Vivian a fairly large trust fund. Now that she's twenty-one she has access. It worries me a little. Fortune hunters, you know."

"Marcus Oliver has his own money. That shouldn't be the reason they're dating, if they are."

He shrugged. "Maybe. I've heard rumors that father and son have gone through a lot of money recently. Louise would never say so, but I think she's having second thoughts about the partnership. She's been more cordial to me of late."

I made no reply. As long as she left Shac alone, I didn't care who Louise might or might not be interested in.

"But she doesn't like to sever ties with anyone she's ever been connected to. Even Shac, as I'm sure you know."

I still kept silent. I had less than no wish to discuss Louise's first ex-husband with her second ex-husband.

He must have finally taken the hint. He stood up, shook my hand, and I ushered him out my office door.

I turned out lights, went back down the hall to my living quarters and finally had my cup of chamomile tea. It didn't help calm the many questions I still had no answers to about the two missing young women. I devoutly hoped the second one would not also turn up dead.

Fourteen

I slept in later than usual next morning. Brought the Sunday paper in and lingered over my cereal and coffee as I paged through it. About eleven I took the paper to my office, intending to read it more carefully.

The entry bell sounded as I stood in front of the bubbling aquarium. I was debating the wisdom of buying a few fish to live in it. Live being the operative word. Like Dan, I also sometimes had to be on stakeout for periods of time. And occasionally went out of town for a couple of days. I'd only been gone to Georgia for a day but there might be a time when I'd have to be gone several days. Could fish survive with extra food for a few days? I'd never been one for pets. I supposed fish might be considered pets. Grandpa had a little white Scottie dog for a year or so when we lived with my grandparents in Fallon. But a coyote killed it and he never got a replacement. I figured he knew best, though I'd liked the Scottie and regretted its death.

I decided to shelve the idea of fish for now and answer the door.

Shac stood on the small entry portico, seeming lost in thought until he noticed I'd opened the door. "Back from the wilds of Alabama already?" I stepped back to let him enter.

"Unnecessary trip, as it turns out. Though the woman did admit to doing the tatt. You know the girl's been identified?"

I slumped into my desk chair and he sat in the client chair. "Yeah. My mystery client."

"Don't start with the self-blame. No way you could have known she'd be murdered within hours of coming here."

"I know." I fussed with the blotter, Rolodex, pottery mug with pens and pencils on my desk. Aligned them all in a straight line. I could see he was still preoccupied with something. But I was determined not to pry. If he wanted to tell me, he would.

"Don said to apologize to you again. He hated acting like a jerk-off with you."

I waved it away. "Tawson ordered him to bring me in. He followed protocol."

He grinned, almost like the Shac I was used to. "Said you told him you wouldn't complain to me that he took your bag. So he told me."

"I knew he would. That's Don."

"Yeah. He said you asked what was on my mind, too."

"I did. But was sorry I had. I don't want to get between you and your partner. You're too good together. Got each other's back."

He seemed to gather his thoughts, make a decision. "Vivian Taggert is missing. Louise asked me to look into it, unofficially. She's twenty-one, and only been out of touch a couple of days."

Again that chill skittering down my spine. Two local girls missing, one now known to be dead, neither known to be missing when the first girl's body was found. What connection, if any, was there between the twenty-one year old step-daughter of a prominent local attorney and the daughter of an executive at a local industry? Then again they most likely frequented the same places, moved in the same social circles.

"Are Louise and Taggert on good terms, then?" Damn. I'd promised myself I'd never bad-mouth Shac's ex-wife to him, even after she came to my condo last year and warned me to leave him alone. Which had led me to consider that she might be the person threatening my life. Subsequent events had proved she wasn't. She'd even informed me that she and Shac were thinking of reuniting. Which had not happened and I was pretty it'd never happen. Would Shac consider the unspoken suggestion that Louise might not be concerned if her stepdaughter was in trouble as bad-mouthing? I hoped not.

His reply brought me back to the present. "I guess. Enough that she said he asked her what to do. He's just out of rehab, wanting to get closer to his daughter. She wouldn't visit him in rehab."

"Bummer. I hope she's okay. Any leads?"

He hesitated. "The case Jake and the Task Force are investigating in Georgia. The girl found behind the convenience store fits her age and general description. DNA is being run, we'll know then if it's her or not."

I'd been doodling again with a pencil from the mug. It snapped in two in my hand. Shac glanced over in surprise, but I ignored it. Let him think it was his mention of the dead girl in Georgia that caused my hand to clench. Which was the case but not in the way he probably assumed.

God, please, no. Not another Wexler Bend parent having to be told his daughter was dead, murdered. Was I obligated to tell Nathan Taggert that the police were looking into that possibility? Or to tell Shac that Nathan, Vivian's biological parent, had retained me to look for her? Don't think about that now.

I had assumed the body found behind the convenience store in Roswell was that of a Georgia girl. I couldn't believe it was Vivian Taggert. Vivian was twenty-one, surely not naive as a teenager, wouldn't fall into the hands of predators so easily.

I'd also assumed, on no evidence, that those who trafficked young girls only took the younger ones, fourteen, fifteen, sixteen and, even more horrible, children.

"Does she have any ties to Georgia?" I finally asked.

"No. Likes to go clubbing in Knoxville. Been seen at some of the seedier ones as well as popular trendy clubs."

"Social girl."

"Active, too. Runs marathons, Black belt in Tae Kwon Do."

"Well, I guess that's in her favor. She can take care of herself. Boyfriend?" I thought about Mindy/Selena hiring me to find her boyfriend. And then another thought struck me. I must have made a sound and I know I slapped the desk.

"What?" Shac asked sharply.

"I forgot to tell Tawson about the big roll of cash the Goren girl was carrying. She just peeled two hundred dollar bills off as casually as I would ones."

"Want me to tell him?"

"I'd better. I said I'd let him know if I thought of anything else." Not that I especially wanted to talk to Shac's boss. Not many people could put me on the defensive anymore, but he could.

"Selena's father is a senior executive at Southern, but their finances are stretched to the limit." Shac seemed to be thinking out loud. "She drove an expensive car, wore real diamonds and designer clothes. Mother probably does, too. Could explain the financial picture. But where did she get all that cash?"

"Drug dealing? Not just a mule?"

"And is the cash in the river or did the killer take it?" Shac wondered aloud.

Before we got too deep into throwing ideas around, I called Captain Tawson's private number.

He answered on the second ring. "Yes?"

"Cam Locke." I said. "I'm calling to let you know I forgot to tell you something last evening."

"What?"

"The Goren girl was carrying a wad of cash in her purse when she came to my office. She took the two hundred dollar bills for the retainer off of it."

"How much would you guess?"

I brought up an image of the roll of bills. "Several thousand, I'd say."

"Did she mention anything about it, reason she had it?"

"No. Just casually pulled it out."

"And you didn't ask her, I suppose?"

I laughed. "Hardly. But I did wonder about it."

"You've told Detective Lane."

"Yes." Someone else must have been with him. He didn't usually refer to Shac so formally with me.

"Thank you. Let me know if you remember anything else." He hung up.

68

Shac left without my having told him that Nathan Taggert was a client. That he'd hired me to do what Louise had asked him to do, unofficially. In the absence of definitive identification of the dead girl in Georgia as Vivian, I didn't see that it was necessary. I'd have to deal with how he saw it when and if the time came.

I turned on my computer and this time was able to renew my subscription to the database I'd been trying to access since Wednesday. Selena Goren had been identified and the case was now definitely a homicide, to be investigated by the police. But I was still curious as to what might turn up in the background of her parents.

The website did reveal information about Robert Goren and his wife, Alva. Robert, son of a civic bean counter in Decatur, had interned with Southern Moldings while a senior at the University of Alabama. When he'd earned his BS, he was hired as a mid-level manager. After marrying Alva six months after graduation and during the next eighteen years he climbed the corporate ladder. Alva had grown up in a small town near Birmingham, father a laborer, mother a homemaker. They seemed to always live just beyond their means, but no serious financial problems until they moved to Wexler Bend. They were at present three months behind on their mortgage.

Little bells began pinging in my head. Whatever I might or might not need to tell Shac about my involvement in searching for Vivian Taggert, I was obligated to ask if he knew about the Goren financial problems. Then I remembered that he had mentioned that fact when he sat in my office earlier. It was almost a certainty that he'd found out the same way I had. And he had access to much broader sources of information. He must be considering, as I was, the question of whether Selena's father would have involved his own daughter in moving drugs to get him out from under financial distress. Or her mother. Women were fully capable of despicable acts, as I well knew. Still I felt I had to check.

I dialed Shac's cell phone, but when the ring tone ended I got the service's unwelcome, canned message that 'this subscriber is out of range. Please try later.'

Now I really needed to get to work on the job I'd been hired to do, look for Vivian Taggert. I printed out my file on my interview with her father and noted the address of Vivian's workplace. She was an assistant manager at *Vicki's on Lyn*, an upscale dress shop on Lyn Street. But today being Sunday the shop would be closed. Her home address was familiar. Wexler Pointe Condos, my own last address. Might as well start there.

I stopped first by her condo, but as Nathan had said, there was no answer when I rang her doorbell. I walked around the side and tried the back doorbell and the doorknob. No answer, of course, and the door was locked as tight as the front. My next stop was the condominium's office. Their turnover in office staff was always in flux and I didn't know the young woman unlucky enough to be on duty. And she did not know anything about Vivian Taggert's whereabouts. As far as she knew, Vivian paid her condo fees in a timely manner, kept the areas of her home visible to the public in an acceptable appearance. The Association was a stickler for that. I knew that for a fact. The girl also had no idea, she said, if Vivian was in the habit of having friends over, for visits or overnight. The Association didn't care as long as no minors were brought in to live permanently as there was an age requirement in the Condo Covenants.

I got back in my car and sat for a few moments, thinking. I could look up the owner or owners of the dress shop and call them. They probably would not be happy to be disturbed on a Sunday afternoon. But they would know if Vivian had shown up for work on Saturday. Since clothing stores were usually open on Saturday, I was assuming

Vicki's on Lyn was and she might have been scheduled to work.

However when I returned to the office and found the after hours number for the shop, there was no answer. So, I'd have to go there tomorrow. I could talk to her manager and fellow employees, if I went in person.

I gave up the search for the day and started to do some mundane chores of living. A little dusting, laundry. A more thorough reading of the newspaper over a deli ham and cheese I'd picked up on the way home.

I'd noted the hours of operation for *Vicki's on Lyn* on Sunday so I arrived a few minutes after the doors opened Monday morning. An anorexic-looking young woman pounced as soon as I entered. Her bronze-tinted name tag spelled out 'Yvonne' in elaborate cursive. I looked at a couple of overpriced teddys, then asked if she knew Vivian.

She immediately glanced over her shoulder and lowered her voice. "If she's a friend of yours, you'd better tell her she's in big trouble. Mr. Zarnes is on the warpath after she didn't show up for work Saturday and again today."

"She was scheduled to work Saturday and today?"

"Yes. And didn't call in sick or anything. Today was my day off, but I'm glad to get the overtime."

A man emerged from the back of the shop. He looked to be in his late thirties but there were only sparse strands of hair on the top of his head. He ran a hand through them and stared toward me and the clerk I was talking with.

"That's the manager, I'd better get to work." But the girl didn't seem concerned that her manager stared at her. She arranged the teddies so they were evenly spaced on the rack before she drifted away.

The manager of *Vicki's on Lyn*, Herb Zarnes, according to the clerk, walked to meet me and said, "Can I help you, Miss, Ms –?"

"Cameron Locke. Ms. I'll just take a moment of your time, Mr. Zarnes."

"That's all I have. I'm having to run everything myself today."

"I'd like to ask you about your assistant manager, Vivian Taggert. Do -"

Angry words erupted from Zarnes before I could finish. "I have a few questions for Ms. Taggert myself. She was supposed to be here, it's my day off. If you see her, tell her she'll very likely not be working here in future."

"So she didn't ask for the day off, herself?"

"No. And she wouldn't have got it if she had. I had plans." Zarnes began rearranging gauzy blouses on a nearby rack. "Is that all?"

"Does she have a boyfriend? If so, might she be with him?"

"I have absolutely no idea. I do not wish to know all about my employees' personal lives." But I caught his surreptitious glance at the slender young woman I'd been speaking to.

"Thank you. May I leave my card with you in case you think of something that might help me locate Ms. Taggert?"

He hesitated, but did take my card, turned on his heel and walked back toward the rear of the store.

I'd just reached the corner of Lyn and Wexler Boulevard when a dark green Lexus SUV turning onto Lyn almost scraped my left front fender. The driver scowled at me as though it was my fault. We recognized each other at the same moment and I'm sure our scowls were a perfect match.

Louise Taggert. I would have given odds on a bet that she was headed for the place I'd just left, *Vicki's on Lyn*. She wouldn't be content to let Shac do the investigating any more than I would, I unwillingly acknowledged. Though I couldn't actually imagine that Louise Taggert had much affection for anyone, especially a stepdaughter. I supposed I should give her a little benefit of doubt that it was possible. I was more inclined to the cynical opinion that it was the money Vivian had inherited from her grandfather that attracted Louise's fondness, if any.

Given Louise Taggert's propensity for confrontations I figured there was a good chance I could expect a visit from her later. I drove home and ate an early lunch of corn chips and a boiled egg at my desk to fortify myself for my expected visitor.

Then I entered notes on my interviews at *Vicki's-on-Lyn* for my file on Vivian Taggert. Nathan had left a message on my answering machine asking for an update, at my convenience. I called him to report my progress, or lack of. I didn't tell him the more time that went by with no information on her whereabouts the more concerned I was.

I was considering whether to call Shac on the chance that he would tell me if he'd heard anything on the DNA results from Georgia. I knew that Nathan, as Vivian's father, would be informed first so most likely no information was available yet. Maybe I just wanted to hear his voice. I squelched any more thoughts along that line. The sound of my office doorbell put a period to it.

At the same time a small picture appeared on my computer's monitor. I mentally high-fived myself. I pressed the house intercom button for my office door and said, "Can I help you?"

"I doubt it, but I want a word with you, Ms. Locke."

Louise had arrived on schedule.

Seventeen

Under my desk my toe pressed the button that was set in the floor to unlock the outside door. "The door is unlocked now. Come in, Louise." I sang out.

She strode through the entrance foyer and straight to my desk. She threw something down on the blotter. My business card. I hadn't risen and I didn't ask her to sit but she didn't wait for an invitation.

"How do you have the nerve to go around my daughter's workplace, asking questions that are none of your business?"

I shrugged and replied lightly. "Ex-stepdaughter."

Her face turned red and her mouth gaped. "What?"

"Vivian Taggert is, or was, your stepdaughter. When you were married to her father."

"And what is that distinction to you, you gumshoe wannabe?"

"I'll leave aside the fact that I am a licensed private investigator, not a 'wannabe.' The distinction means that she is a presumed competent adult and not your offspring. I have no reason to think you adopted an eighteen-year-old woman, so you have no grounds to question my inquiries about her." I delivered this speech in the tone of an instructor on the finer points of a subject.

Her response to my lecture was interesting to observe. Her face achieved a deeper shade of crimson and her small eyes seemed to shrink even more as they narrowed in anger. Her mouth opened and closed a couple of times. She had the reputation of an excellent litigator, an opponent to be wary of in the courtroom. But apparently even tough lawyers could be tripped up by their personal biases and hates. I had no illusions about her extreme aversion to me. Baiting someone like Louise Taggert was not a wise move on my part probably. I waited to see what zinger she would eventually come up with.

"You must have snooped and found out I'd asked Shac, my ex-husband, with whom I am on good terms, by the way, to make sure Vivian is okay."

"You asked him?" I emphasized the 'you'. "What about her father?"

"That is none of your business either. I'm ordering you to cease and desist bothering Vivian's friends and co-workers."

I laughed. "Ordering?"

She was silent for a moment. Her hands clenched and unclenched a couple of times and she pressed her lips together in an apparent attempt to rein in her fury. She looked around the office and her gaze settled on the bubbling aquarium. Then her attention returned to me and she seemed to be considering something.

"You wouldn't be prying into Vivian's affairs on your own. There'd be no pay. Shac wouldn't have asked you to do what he can do better. So why?"

I saw understanding dawn on her. "Nathan." She suddenly rose from her chair. "He'll regret this. How the hell can you bewitch both my dim-witted ex-husbands?"

Sure. I bewitched Nathan from afar and drew him to my office so he would hire me to look for his daughter. I wondered how said ex-husbands would react to hearing her opinion of them. I could arrange that, but I wouldn't. No one knew about the sophisticated, and automatic, digital AV recording system Dan had installed in his office. It normally was written over daily, but any segment could be retrieved before it was.

Louise jerked her Gucci bag over her shoulder and stalked to the door without another word. She tried to slam the door but was defeated by the pneumatic closer. The automatic lock would prevent her re-entry in case she thought of some other accusation to hurl at me.

I stared at the area on the wall with an invisible panel behind which resided the recording equipment. A few clicks and a password protected program on my computer would pull the recording of the last half hour in seconds. I resisted the strong temptation but not without effort. I refused to stoop to her level. Shac might or might not still have a remnant of feeling for the wife who threw him over for a more expensive, though drunken, model. He would have to decide that on his own.

Instead I decided to do some discreet inquiries on Louise Taggert's law partner. I only knew him by sight and local reputation. Nathan had said he thought Louise harbored some regrets about the partnership. I hadn't given the possibility much attention as it was so much Louise's modus operandi. Suck what she could from a relationship and then get rid of the schmuck. Though I doubted many people would characterize Marcus Oliver as a schmuck. Raised in the rarified circles of the state judicial circuit in Nashville he could and did get by with almost anything.

I wanted to refresh my limited memory about the trouble that had caused his father to banish him to the hinterlands of Wexler Bend. When I found it, I wondered how I had forgotten. A girl, a young woman about seventeen, had been sexually assaulted and thrown from the back door of a car. Her injuries were severe. An investigative reporter had been in the ER on another story when she was brought in, almost dead. She briefly regained some consciousness as the police attempted to question her. The reporter heard her name a judge's son as one of her assailants.

A witness who saw her dumped from the car got a partial license plate number which confirmed the car belonged to the judge's son. The witness refused to back down even in the face of reported threats on his life. Eventually a friend of the son was identified as the driver and he swore Marcus Oliver was passed out in the front seat. Another friend was in the back seat with the girl. The second friend was tried and when found guilty, sentenced to a year in prison, paroled after a few months. He left the state after his release. The girl had also left Tennessee immediately after the trial.

Even so the scandal tainted the Nashville political scene enough that there was talk of impeachment on grounds of obstruction of justice. The judge sent his son, Marcus Oliver, as far from the capital as possible and still remain in the state. There was speculation in the press that the judge wanted his son to remain in the state so that he could keep eyes and ears on him.

I sat back to catch my breath. How could I have been so oblivious to the horrific history of Louise Taggert's law partner? How could even she stand to be in the same firm with him? Apparently the year of working with Dan, then struggling to get my PI business going followed by a case that nearly cost my life had consumed me to the exclusion of all else. At least I now knew how, most likely, Louise had been able to set up that lavish office suite in the Clare View office complex. After yesterday's meeting with Nathan when he retained me to look for Vivian, I knew she hadn't gotten enough from their divorce to finance the law practice. And certainly her divorce from a lowly police detective had netted her pennies, if that.

But the Olivers were another story. Reputedly for sale to the highest bidder, the elder Nashville jurist owned extensive property in Davidson County, which included a mansion in Bell Meade, a busy, prosperous shopping mall, a large horse farm. Who said you couldn't make a darned good living in the judicial profession. I guess it depended on which laws you adjudicated.

And then the implications of the story I'd just read hit me full force. Thinking about Nathan reminded me that he'd suspected Vivian was dating Marcus Oliver. But the girl in Nashville he'd been accused of almost killing was a teenager. Vivian was a fit twenty-one-year old young woman. Surely she could hold her own against anyone who threatened her. Given warning, of course, a little voice in my head whispered. I'd known what to expect from Emory Locke, since I'd endured it enough times, the day I decided to use my self-defense training and stood up to him. Vivian was a beautiful young woman, but traffickers, I would have thought, didn't choose young women trained in martial arts to kidnap and sell into sexual slavery.

When I realized where my thoughts were going, my blood ran cold. Was I actually considering that one of the top judges in the state and his son were involved in that horrible business? Bad enough that the son had almost killed a girl. I believed he had, even if someone else took the blame, and was handsomely paid to do it, I was sure.

I bookmarked the latest site I'd been reading and switched off the monitor. I'd noticed a couple of articles linked from the local Wexler Bend paper. But I had to get out in the fresh air. Just reading these stories and my speculations made me want to close my office and never have to even think of such things again.

Eighteen

I did leave the office, after making sure the alarm was set. In my bedroom I donned old jeans, and hiking boots. Clare Creek Mountain had been my refuge from stress for years. I had to go to my favorite place there, take solace from that stubborn patch of yellow roses.

When I had negotiated the several switchbacks up the mountain I waved at Fern when I arrived at the gate, and she motioned me on through. I parked in the upper lot above the Nature Museum. I got out of the car and did a few stretches, just to relieve kinks, I didn't plan to do any strenuous hiking. I set off up the paved path, enjoying the trees and their new spring green leaves. Thankfully, being almost killed when the senator's psycho wife threw me over the reservoir dam had not permanently turned off my love for the park.

I had walked a half-mile or so and just stepped off the path to approach the area of the old homestead left behind by the park's original owner when I heard engines behind me. I looked around. ATV's were not allowed in the park. The prohibition did not apply to police ATV's apparently. Two roared up behind me, blue lights flashing, and a voice over a loudspeaker spoke to me. At least I was the only person I had observed in the area.

"Please return to the path, Ma'am. This is a police matter. Do not move further off the path."

What the -? A three wheeled motorcycle moved up behind the ATV's and two people dismounted. I stepped back on the path and waited. After pausing to don blue plastic booties over their shoes, uniformed officers, some of whom I recognized, spread out along the path, eyes on the ground. One dropped a yellow triangle on the spot where I'd stepped off the path.

Jake Hunter had been a passenger on the lead ATV and seemed to be directing the activities of the officers, ignoring me as though I weren't there. Shac and Taylor Glass wove their way up the path toward me.

Taylor nodded. 'Not exactly *déjà vu*, but close, huh, Cam?"

"What are you doing here, Cam?" Shac demanded.

As usual he managed to get my back up with his first words. "The last I heard Clare Creek Mountain was a public park," I snapped.

"But why now, today?"

"Why all this police activity? The murdered girl was found down by the river."

Just then somebody called him and he gave me a 'this is not all' look before turning away.

"Still hung-up on each other, I see," Taylor remarked.

I barked a laugh. "You think? Since you and Jake are here, I could hazard a guess as to the reason for all this. Or will you tell me?"

She gave me a measuring look. She opened her mouth to reply, but a tall young guy wearing a windbreaker with TBI in large letters on the back walked up and touched her shoulder. He handed her a clear plastic evidence bag. She thanked him and he left. She studied the plastic bag for a few seconds, then held it up so I could see the contents. "Recognize it?"

The bag held a flower, a yellow rose. "You know I do." I pointed. "They grow right over there. Where I was headed when I was ordered back to the path."

"Why were you going there?" Her voice was level, no inflection.

"It's where I go when I'm in need of serenity and comfort." I replied. There was probably a touch of asperity in my voice. I might be only a lowly private investigator, but I'd helped law enforcement before. Surely I didn't have to justify my every action when I was minding my own business.

"You weren't following a lead on a case?" Her question was still couched in a level tone.

"What lead? I was taking a break from sitting in an office chair. What do these roses have to do with the Task Force investigation?"

"Go home, or wherever, for now, Cam. We'll talk later at the station." She wagged a 'come here' gesture at the tall young man in the TBI windbreaker. "Maybe we can go to the range for some target practive while I'm here." I just looked at her, not knowing how to answer.

When the guy in the windbreaker reached her, she said, "Please take Ms. Locke back down to the parking lot and see that she drives off the mountain. Use the three-wheeler."

She turned to another officer who had walked up and said something to her. The young agent touched my arm. I moved away, but not before I noticed that his badge was not TBI or Wexler Bend, city or county. If I was not mistaken, it said Nashville Police Department. His expression was grim and hard for such a young man. I wondered if dreadful things he'd seen in a surely not very long career, given his apparent age, had spawned the hardness. If so he probably would not last, would burn out.

The only words we exchanged on the way to the parking lot were when I pointed out my car, unnecessarily, since it was now the only one there. The few cars that had been in the lot when I arrived were now gone. He touched his cap when I left the three-wheeler and walked to my car. He even drove behind me through the lot.

As we moved through the lower parking lot, yellow crime scene tape blocked two of the traffic lanes and effectively barred access to the path leading to the dam. A path I remembered well and had not ventured onto for a year. I tried and failed to think of some reason connected to the homicide of a young girl not too far from the base of the mountain to account for the police action on the mountain. I supposed my strong wish to understand it would have to wait until someone read me into it, if they ever did.

The officer tailed me all the way to the gate. To make sure I left the mountain, I guessed.

When I reached the gate I saw that more crime scene tape now barred the entry drive. And a Wexler Bend police cruiser was parked across it, light bar activated.

I switched on my scanner, tuned it to the police frequency, but heard only normal traffic, a fender bender code, a possible domestic assault. Any discussion concerning whatever was being investigated atop Clare Creek Mountain was no doubt going out over an encrypted channel.

It was late afternoon when I arrived back at my office, still puzzling over the police activity on the mountain. The message light on my office phone was blinking. The time stamp indicated I'd just missed the call. I listened to it with a heavy heart.

Nathan Taggert's voice was rough with emotion. It sounded as though he was talking through tears. "Cam. Vivian's dead. Captain Tawson and a police counselor came to tell me. Her body was found in Atlanta." He stopped talking for a moment. I heard noise which sounded as though he was blowing his nose. "What was she doing in Atlanta? Did you learn anything that might say why? Cam, I'm trying my best not to go and pick up a bottle of Scotch. Please call me."

I cut the message off, though he was still talking, and punched in his number. His phone rang only twice before he answered, but I had time to see him in my mind's eye at the liquor store, a clerk putting the bottle of Scotch in a fancy long bag.

"Cam? Thank God. Are you at your office?"

"Yes, Nathan. I am so sorry. Is anyone with you? Do you want me to come?"

"Can I come to your office? She wasn't here much, but it still reminds me of her."

"Of course. And, Nathan ..." I stopped. Telling an alcoholic not to pick up a bottle was not guaranteed to achieve that end.

"I won't." He knew what I'd been about to blurt out. "But I need to talk to somebody or I will. I'll hate it, but I will."

"I could come and bring you here. You're pretty upset to be driving."

"I can do it. Just be there. Okay?"

I assured him I would. I wondered if Louise knew. Had he called her? I turned on the Bunn coffee maker and roamed around the room, finally winding up at the window. I let my thoughts wander where they would.

Dan's landscaped yard was beginning to need the ministrations of the gardening company he'd used. I should call them. Some of the stones edging flower beds had been dislodged. When I'd lived in the condo the Association had taken care of all outside landscaping. This ownership of a free standing house was new to me. Should get a handle on it. So much death. Was I in the wrong profession? Dan had assured me that long stakeouts without handy restroom facilities was about the hardest thing about being a PI. His own murder had given the lie to that assurance. I heard a car turn into my drive and dropped that line of thought. It would not help me console Nathan Taggert. If that was even possible.

Nineteen

I crossed to the door and opened it as he stepped up to the recessed entry. I took his hand and drew him into the office. Even though we'd been acquaintances for years, I didn't feel I knew him well enough for a comforting embrace. "Coffee?"

"Please. Black." He dropped into the client chair. Put his head in his hands.

He raised his head when I brought his coffee, eyes brimming. "If you love someone, Cam, tell them. You don't know when it will be too late. I wasted so much time. And now she's gone."

Did I love anyone? I'd loved my father and he died. I loved my mother and she'd died, too. Or was murdered, maybe, like Vivian. I thought her death had hurt me more. Maybe it would help me help Nathan. My driving need to know what Tawson had told him about the circumstances of Vivian's death had to wait.

He drank coffee, lost in his own regrets, it seemed. Perhaps regrets for not being there for Vivian when she was growing up, letting the bottle take him away from her. I didn't intrude, no one could face them for him. He just needed to be with someone. He had apparently not reached out to Louise, but I could understand that. I couldn't imagine Louise providing comfort to anyone.

Thoughts of Louise led to Shac. Did I love Shac? If I did, why did the mental image of Jake Hunter sometimes overshadow my thoughts of him? Maybe I should forget any ideas of romance with either man. They were police detectives. And law enforcement was one of the most dangerous professions. To love a police officer was to court heartbreak. But Dan had died, I almost had, was there no safety anywhere?

Nathan sighed and set his cup on my desk. "I'll need to go to a meeting in a little while. But I couldn't be alone. Thanks, Cam."

"You're welcome." I hesitated. "If you want to talk, go ahead. Or ask me anything about my investigation, though I've little to tell you."

"Please tell me what you have."

"She didn't tell anyone at work that she was not coming in, on Saturday or today. She was scheduled both days."

"Tawson didn't tell me much. After they left I drove to her condo. They were there, too, and wouldn't let me go in. Does that mean she was murdered?"

I tried to keep a noncommittal expression on my face. Was there a connection between the sudden appearance of police and Task Force members on Clare Creek Mountain and Vivian's death? How could there be? And how did she get to Atlanta? The tattoo artist Shac had tracked to Atlanta and then Alabama had been connected to Selena Goren, not Vivian. What didn't I know? A lot it seemed.

"I don't know, Nathan. I haven't been told anything, by Shac or anyone, about Vivian. Other than the fact that she was missing. Louise had asked him to look into it, find out if she was gone voluntarily or not. That was Sunday. Yesterday."

"Louise!" The way he spit out her name was the first time he'd shown real animosity toward his ex-wife. "I was worried enough that I actually called her to see if she knew anything. And asked her what I should do."

I waited to see if he would elaborate.

"She tried to insinuate herself into Vivian's life, get between us after the divorce. Pretended a motherly interest, but Vivian wasn't buying it. She had Louise's number from the beginning."

No surprise there. Vivian telegraphed her sole interest in turning everything to her advantage. I regretfully decided she wasn't involved in Vivian's death since there was no way I could see that she would profit from it.

But what about her law partner? Did Nathan know about Marcus Oliver's history? I decided not to mention it. If there was a connection between Oliver and Vivian the police would find it and ask Nathan if he knew about it. Time enough then to add to his sorrow.

Nathan left for his Twelve Step meeting around five-thirty. Still in my office I was considering what I might come up with to serve as dinner when my phone rang. The caller ID showed the Wexler Bend Police Department's main number. I snatched up the phone. "Cameron Locke Investigations."

"Taylor, Cam. Will you come down to the station, please?" Well, she did say 'please.' I stifled a feeling suspiciously akin to disappointment that the summons had not come from Shac or Jake. Knowing myself I also suspected that even if it had, I would have found something to resent in the way they phrased the request.

For God's sake, give it a rest, I told myself. Maybe they had found some evidence on the mountain to help find the killer or killers of at least one of the young women.

I punched the rocker switch beside the door, leaving only the aquarium lights on in the office, made sure the alarm was set and went out to my car. I clicked the remote to unlock the car door and heard a step behind me in the gravel. I started to turn and something crashed into the side of my head. I felt my bag drop from my grasp as light from the security lamp on its tall pole abruptly faded to black.

Excruciating pain lanced through my head when I opened my eyes. A loud noise was sounding somewhere out of my field of vision, such as it was. It sounded familiar, but I couldn't place it.

"She's coming around." Someone said above and behind me. Maybe so, but all in all I would have preferred to go back to wherever I was before the pain.

Shac's face loomed above me. "Cam? Cam? Can you see me? Say something."

"I will, if you'll give me a chance. What happened?"

Relief registered on the face of the man I tried so often to decide whether or not I was maybe a little in love with.

89

"You don't remember? We found you lying in the grass, with a head injury."

"Detective, we really need to get her to the hospital. Head injuries are dangerous, need to be x-rayed to rule out a skull fracture."

Being a detective myself, I realized now that I was lying on a gurney-slash-stretcher. And the person speaking to Shac was most likely a paramedic. Where was Taylor, to repeat her mantra, *'déjà vu, Cam.'* Of course, she hadn't been there immediately when I'd stumbled into the arms of a security agent on Clare Creek Mountain after my treacherous climb up the steps of the dam.

"Will someone please turn that noise off?" My voice sounded querulous to my own ears.

Shac touched my face. "Sure, if you can remember the security code."

I struggled to bring the code to mind and gave it to him. He disappeared and in a moment the annoying noise stopped. The paramedics took advantage of his absence to get me to the ambulance parked in the street in front of my house. Don Mears appeared at the back of the ambulance as they strapped the gurney in place.

"Cam. Are you okay? I heard the radio call."

Shac swung up into the back of the ambulance. "She will be, Don. Hold the fort." One of the techs opened his mouth to speak, but closed it when Shac looked at him and said, "I'm going."

The tech busied himself inserting an IV and Shac held my other hand. "Who's going to find out what happened at my house?" I asked him.

"Taylor, Don, and Jake are there. What do you remember?"

"Not much. Taylor called and I went out to my car to drive down to the station. I heard a step in the gravel and then everything went dark."

"So. Did you piss anybody off today?" But he smiled as he said it. It was supposed to be a funny reference to the question he'd asked me when I'd been the target of a killer last year. I didn't feel like laughing.

At the hospital my head was x-rayed, but no fracture found. "Too hardheaded." Shac told the resident who stitched me up, not the same doctor who'd treated me twice last year. I guessed he'd finished his residency, no doubt thankful I hadn't shown up again while he was still there.

The young doctor said what I expected, that I should stay at the hospital overnight for observation. I declined. "Then somebody will need to stay with you. In case you go into a coma and don't wake up." He then went into the standard recitation of all the things that could result from a head injury.

"She won't be alone." Shac interrupted. "We've been through this before. If she passes out I'll bring her back."

"All right, then." He handed me the release papers to sign, said he was writing a prescription for a mild pain medication. If I didn't hate to beg, I would have asked for a script for a strong one.

We both realized when we passed through the automatic ER exit doors that we had no transportation. At that moment, Don Mears pushed away from the entrance pillars. "Need taxi service?" He grinned. "There'll be a double charge for two, of course."

"Stuff it." Shac grunted. "Where is everyone?"

"Cam's house. Jake and Taylor didn't figure it would look too good to haul her down to the station when she's an invalid and all. But they want to talk to her, if she's up to it."

"You can stuff the invalid characterization of my condition, too, Mears." I said. "You're on thin ice, still."

Don was driving Shac's beat-up Kia squad car and insisted I lie down in the back seat. I did not argue much, to his obvious surprise. I took advantage of the quarter hour ride to try and think why someone would knock me out in my own driveway. No reason had occurred to me by the time we pulled up in front of my house.

Twenty

When we filed inside, my living room seemed filled with people, several of whom I did not know. They seemed to have made themselves at home. Cardboard take out cups and plates littered every surface. Pizza boxes were stacked neatly by the door and sandwich wrappers filled waste baskets.

Taylor Glass stepped forward, eyeing my bandage-wrapped head. "How do you feel?"

"About as well as I look," I replied. "What have you found out?"

"Let me introduce you to some other members of the Task Force. We really wanted to talk to you, but it didn't feel right to ask you to come to the station after your attack."

"Appreciate it. Hope you found everything you need." I said, half meaning it anyway.

Taylor led me to a middle-aged man who carried a few extra pounds. "Cameron Locke, this is Oren Bedner. Oren is our IT expert."

My face must have shown the spear of alarm that shot through me. Surely they wouldn't have snooped into my computer system. Taylor gave a small laugh. "Don't worry, Cam. Your secrets are safe – for now."

I wasn't sure what she meant but had no time to decide. She introduced me to the other members of the Task Force who were present. Arthur Waters was a twenty-year veteran sex crimes detective from Miami/Dade PD. Ben Price had joined the Task Force on loan from Birmingham Major Crimes. The two remaining members were in Georgia, still working with the GBI and Atlanta PD on Vivian Taggert's murder, trying to determine if it was connected to sex trafficking.

Bedner returned to clicking keys on the laptop open on my coffee table. Waters and Price alternated texting on their iPhones and surfing for information on their iPads. Jake came in from the kitchen and began gathering up cups and plates.

"Coffee is hot, Cam, if you'd like a cup. Contraindications?".He looked at Shac and raised an eyebrow.

"Nah. She mainlines it." Shac guided me to my favorite chair.

Jake went to the kitchen and returned with a steaming mug which he placed on the table beside me. "My favorite mug."

"I noticed." It was one I'd ordered from a catalog the same time I'd ordered Shac's, which had a handcuffs graphic on it. Mine was imprinted with a stylized female form, holding a disproportionately large magnifying glass.

I glanced up to see if Shac had heard, but he was speaking with Taylor. I hoped they'd get down to business before I conked out, despite the strong coffee, from the pain pill I'd swallowed in the ER.

Tuesday morning I opened my eyes and wondered why a lamp was on in my bedroom when I was in bed. Wearing my favorite disreputable, polka dot, paper-thin flannel pajamas. I jerked straight up in bed. How had I gotten here? Who undressed me? The last thing I remembered I was fighting to stay awake in my easy chair while the Task Force members, who had taken over my house, dug for clues to the identity of Selena's and Vivian's killer or killers. And whether they were part of the same case.

Shac stuck his head around the doorway. "Sleeping Beauty awake?"

"How ..." I waved my hand.

"Don't worry. Your virtue is intact." He put on an exaggerated leer. "Taylor managed to get you into your jammies. I had to leave the lamp on so I could check on you during the night."

I touched the bandage on the side of my head. I hadn't noticed but my head wasn't hurting. The night's rest had done its work.

"She said she'd call you later about that trip to the range, if you're up to it," he added.

I smelled coffee as Shac came on into the room holding my mug. "Didn't know if you'd want to eat. I can do toast."

I took a sip of coffee. "No, this is fine. Thanks." I didn't worry about him seeing me in the ratty pajamas. He'd seen them before.

He sat on the side of the bed and grabbed my left foot. "Wiggle your toes."

"Wiggle my toes? Why should I?"

"Cam. I have to check to see if the damage to your head had any effect on the rest of you."

"I don't believe that. You made it up."

He put on the wolfish leer again. "I did. You see, I have this strange toe fetish."

His leer vanished and I'm sure my expression mirrored my dismay as the nature of the case that challenged us came back with intensity to both of us.

He was silent for a moment, patting my foot absently. He finally spoke. "Do you want to get up?"

"I certainly do. Where's the Task Force?"

"Went back to their hotel when they left here. We'll convene at the station at one o'clock."

I finished the last of my coffee and set the mug on my nightstand. "Why do you think they're sharing with me? I'm not part of the Task Force."

"Probably because they need your cooperation. This case or cases have given them their best leads. How much do you remember from last night?"

I thought about it. "The GBI lab identified organic material, a flower, found on Vivian's body that was from Clare Creek Mountain Park. They believe she was taken from there and transported to the Atlanta area."

"Uh huh. What else?"

"Did I hear something about a shoe?"

"Someone found an expensive sandal behind the convenience store dumpster. Turned it in."

"The Task Force thinks it might be hers?"

"Maybe. It was found Sunday. But no record of a purchase by her of a pair of those shoes in Georgia. No store in Wexler Bend carries them."

"Nearest place?" Of course, anyone could have lost an expensive shoe in metro Atlanta.

"Knoxville."

I nodded. "So if it's hers, she was probably knocked out before being taken to Georgia."

"And tied up, deep indentation marks on wrists and ankles, like narrow rope. None found. Deep bruise on her face. Abrasions on hands. Could be offensive, so when a possible suspect turns up, he may have marks."

"Struck in the face," I thought out loud, "which may, emphasis on may, be similar to the blow to Selena Goren's face."

"Who was also hit in the abdomen. Which caused the balloon suspended in Selena's stomach to rupture and she died when pure heroin flooded her system."

"And the, maybe, comparable blows are the only similarities in the two deaths. No hint of drugs with Vivian?"

"None. Nada. Two balloons were suspended from a lower molar in Selena's mouth. One was intact. Purest, least adulterated powder ever found on the East coast."

I grabbed a handful of the comforter, clenched it as tight as possible. "But the parents knew nothing? How could they not?"

He shrugged. "Too involved in their own marital war and vices. Father drinks to oblivion almost every night, according to the wife. She shops and hobnobs at society luncheons."

Shac's last statement reminded me that I'd meant to pay a visit to Zoey at the Clare View Hotel. As Head of Security for the hotel she could tell me if Goren regularly drank to excess while a guest or at a party there. If I believed Maxie, and I did, I was pretty sure he would have gotten drunk at parties. I understood that Southern had followed

Eastern's pattern in holding company functions in the only fancy hotel in town. I also wanted to find out what Zoey might know about Marcus Oliver since he'd been in Wexler Bend. The hotel restaurant and bar were where Wexler Bend's elite liked to hang out when not at the country club.

Shac glanced at my bedside clock. "If you're feeling chipper, I'm outta here. Some folks have to work and can't lay abed all morning."

I threw a pillow at him. "Get out, then. I need to get dressed. Some folks not on the public's dime do have to work for a living."

"Such gratitude. Be still, my heart."

I stared at him in amazement. A semi-romantic-literary quote from Shac Lane. Of course, he'd probably heard the line in a movie.

He picked up my mug and started toward the door. Turned and gave a two-finger wave. "Don't forget to check back with the doc this afternoon."

Which reminded me. "Wait. I forgot to ask if you found anything that pointed to who hit me?"

"Mears found a rock near the street with blood on it. Matches the rocks bordering some flower beds and it's your blood type. Too rough to get a fingerprint, though."

"So, didn't bring a weapon with him." I said. "Or her."

"Top Chief has asked the county to do extra patrols in the area to supplement ours. And don't be surprised if you see cops keeping an eye on you around town."

I frowned. "I'd rather they kept an eye on the young girls in town. They're the ones being murdered."

"Ummm, a little further to the temple, and a little harder blow, it might have been you, Cam." Worry darkened his already dark green eyes. "Watch yourself."

"Maybe I'll have more security lights installed. Start pissing off the neighbors here. I don't suppose anyone saw anything?"

"So they said, when cops talked to them."

"Okay. Go. I'll be careful."

He did leave then and a few minutes later I heard the front door close. I followed and saw that he had reset the alarm as he left. I didn't know who might have heard me give him the code as I lay on the stretcher. So I changed it and made a mental note to give him the new one next time I saw him.

I took a quick shower, being careful to cover the bandage on my head with a shower cap. Not much to be done with my short dishwater blonde hair. One side now much shorter where the ER nurse had shaved around the injury.

Returning to my bedroom, I picked up my tote bag, which someone, probably Shac, had thoughfully placed beside my bed where I usually kept it. It felt lighter than usual. A cold chill went down my spine. When I looked inside I got colder still. My Glock was not there. I tried to believe that maybe Shac or one of the others had taken it for safekeeping. But he would have told me. I looked in the lower shallow drawer of my nightstand. My spare was still there. Shac knew about it. If he'd taken one, he'd have taken the other. For whatever reason.

Whoever had attacked me must have taken my gun. Why had no one realized it after they converged on my house when the alarm went off? And why had the attacker gone inside anyway? He had my keys to get inside, but without the code to shut off the alarm, only minutes to find whatever he, or she, went inside to find.

No use putting off the inevitable. I called Shac's cell phone. He answered on the first ring. "Miss me already?"

"My Glock is gone."

Silence on the other end for a second. "Damn. I didn't check your bag because I was worried about you. Your other?"

"It's here."

"I just got out of the shower. Be there in fifteen minutes." The line went dead.

Twenty-One

I left my bag on the unmade bed and paced to the living room and back. An idea occurred to me and I went outside to the place next to my car where I'd been struck. The police had powerful flashlights, but nothing equals daylight for seeing things.

Sure enough in a nearby flowerbed I found the small red enamel key ring fob I'd picked up in a second hand shop in Florida when I hitchhiked there as a teenager. The word 'Shalom' was printed in gold letters on it. It meant 'peace' the owner of the shop said. I bought it because I so wanted peace in my life and ever since had always kept it in whatever purse I carried. Shac drove up seconds after I found it. He swore, put it in a plastic evidence bag.

"Not anybody's fault. It was lying among red flowers."

He just looked at me. I led him back inside and to the bedroom. He used a pen to open the top of the bag. "Touch anything inside it?"

"No. They must have dumped the bag rather than rummage through all the junk I carry for the gun. But why put it all back?"

"Delay us finding out it was taken. And it worked." Shac pulled a large plastic bag from his jacket pocket and put the whole bag in it.

"My keys. I need my keys." I said.

"You have a spare set, don't you?"

"Yes, but what about my other stuff? My notebook. Lipstick."

"You don't wear lipstick half the time. Get another notebook. I'll get the bag back to you as soon as possible." He left again, carrying my purse-slash-tote bag encased in plastic. I tried not to imagine what whoever dusted everything for prints would think about my spare tee shirt and panties when they found them. I hoped they'd realize the clothing had been clean before being dumped on the ground.

I went to my office to get another notebook, pens and small digital recorder and put them in another tote bag with my spare keys and Glock.

While there the thought I'd had of adding more light around my house just before being knocked out returned. I looked up an electrical contracting company on the list of useful numbers Dan had left me. He had been the epitome of organization. I told the receptionist what I needed, a couple of additional security light poles, and she made an appointment for one of their men to come out the next day.

While on the phone I remembered an idea I'd been bouncing around. The office had its digital and video recording system. Why not extend that capability to the rest of the house. I found the number for the security company and placed a service request for security cameras throughout the house. The girl who answered the phone transferred my call to a technician whom I had actually met. He had come out once when I still worked for Dan. He didn't know about Dan's death. I sketched the short version and he expressed sympathy.

Only as I was leaving after making a date for the technician to come out and started to reset the new alarm code did I remember I hadn't given it to Shac. I'd probably see him later in the day, I'd give it to him then.

Twenty-Two

Robert Goren shakily replaced the phone and glanced toward the bedroom door. Alva had taken a bottle of brandy to the bedroom when they returned from the mortuary. She had chosen a top of the line casket, lined with silk, lavish flowers for the top, the most expensive services offered. Rob knew they had no money to pay for his little girl's funeral.

He'd siphoned all he could from his accounts at work. For the last few months they'd lived on plastic, but now most of the credit cards were cancelled. Alva knew that. She'd stormed in from the Clare View Saturday afternoon, before the visit from Captain Tawson.

"Declined! All my cards, declined! I was mortified. Louise Taggert oh so graciously picked up the tab for lunch. The mayor's wife, two Board wives. You'd better fix this, Rob. I won't stand for it."

Only fifteen minutes later none of it mattered in the slightest to Rob. Two police detectives rang their door bell. When they came in and sat on the satin-covered living room sofa, they told the parents that their only child, Selena, had been killed. From a drug overdose. That she'd been carrying drugs inside her body for drug dealers. That they'd provided her with a luxury car, an Infiniti, to travel to other states and deliver the drugs. Rob couldn't take it in. How could their baby have been involved in such sordid affairs and him not know about it?

He dealt with it the only way he knew how, by diving into a bottle of vodka. They'd moved around the house in limbo for two days, not knowing what to do. Police came and went. He didn't know what Alva told them. He was too drunk to say much. When they got word that Selena's body was to be released, Alva roused herself and made an appointment with the most expensive funeral home in Wexler Bend. She wanted to take Selena home to Alabama for burial. Rob knew that was not possible. The cost for transporting a body across state lines was exorbitant. Fees. Permits. He couldn't think how they'd pay for a burial in Wexler Bend.

At least his handler left him alone for the two days. If they'd stayed in Alabama, maybe Selena would still be alive. But the men who owned him had let him know there was no choice. They wanted him in Tennessee. But wouldn't tell him why. He despised himself for not being able to defy them. But he couldn't face prison. His uncle in South America had died in a prison.

Now he had been ordered to a meet with his local contact. Why? If only. But he didn't have the courage, even after his daughter's death, maybe at their hands. He picked up the bottle of vodka and finished it. He rose from his chair and went out to get in his car to meet the man.

"The grieving father." The man sneered. "Come in, Mr. Goren."

Rob stumbled a little as he crossed the threshold. He caught the door jamb to regain his balance.

"You'd better sit down before you fall down, greaser."

Rob fell into a chair. "I'm a citizen. Same as you." His words slurred a little. He'd found another bottle he'd forgotten about hiding under the driver's seat of his car.

"Citizen!" The man snorted in fury. "Not bloody likely. I can trace my family back – "

"To colonial days." Rob jeered, in angry sorrow and liquid courage. "Mine goes back to the Conquistadors. While yours were still hawking coal from carts in the streets of -." He didn't have a chance to finish. The other man rushed across the room and knocked him to the floor.

"Where's my money? I own you. I'd take your wife and sell her, but the bitch wouldn't bring a fraction of what the girl would have."

Rob stared up at the man. "It was you. You killed my girl." For the first time he noticed that the whole side of the man's face was mottled and muddy colored, the left eye black and bruised all around. "Did she do that to you before you killed her? If she did she had more courage than I ever had."

"Her?" The man kicked Rob in the side. "Hardly. When she delivered that last shipment she thought you'd be in the clear. But you know even the twenty five thousand I was going to get for her wouldn't have come close."

"You were going to sell my baby girl?" Rob roared, charging from the floor in an adrenaline fueled rage.

The man back-pedaled in sudden fear, picked up the gun on his desk and fired point blank. Freed of his tormentor at last, Rob dropped to the floor and didn't move.

Twenty-Three

I made my way to the By-Pass and drove five miles or so. When I reached the exit for the Clare View Hotel and Conference Center, I left it and turned into the long curving driveway that ended at the Clare View. The Hotel sat in the shadow of Clare Creek Mountain, which gave it its name. This time I elected to go through the main entrance and follow the interior corridors to Zoey's Security Office. Unlike my last visit to Zoey's domain, which almost ended our friendship and ultimately almost ended my life.

Darrell, her rotund second in charge, was eating lunch at the desk in the outer office. I nodded to him as I noticed some changes had been made since I was here last. A bank of six monitors were ranked on the wall beside the desk. By the way the pictures switched I could tell that cameras had been installed at a number of key locations throughout the hotel. Including the staircase I'd sneaked up to avoid the front desk clerk. And came back down wrapped in a rug, unconscious. Some might have called it poetic justice, but I would have to disagree.

"Zoey around, Darrell?" I asked.

"Should be back any minute. Had to check on something. Have a seat, Cam."

"Thanks."

Darrell took another bite of ham sandwich and eyed my head. "Had another run-in with a bad guy—er-woman?"

I smiled and nodded. "Don't know which. Conked on the head in my own driveway, for God's sake."

His question made me think of my missing Glock. Why had my attacker taken my gun? If he, or she, killed someone with it, how would I live with that? I would probably lose my Private Investagator license if that happened. I had to find a way to get it back.

Before I could berate myself too long for losing my gun, Zoey came in the office. Her eyes, too, went immediately to my bandaged head. "Cam. What happened to you now?"

Zoey wasn't one to mince words. But she did seem to be fond of me so she came over and hugged me.

"Are you busy? Can I have a minute?"

She shook her head, presumably meaning she wasn't busy, and said, "Come on in the office." She led the way as we squeezed by the desk and through a door behind it.

"Coffee?" She asked.

"Thanks, no. Think I've had my quota for now."

"Didn't think that was possible," she said. Zoey had been my best officer when I headed security at Eastern Fabricators. Not much got by her sharp black eyes, set in a small face with a beautiful and perfectly smooth mocha complexion.

"Trying to cut back." I took the chair that barely fit in the room with a desk and office chair. A thermal carafe sat on the corner of the desk, flanked by a short stack of cardboard cups and other accoutrements for coffee.

"So. Tell me about that bandage."

I repeated what I'd told Darrell, making a light story of it, as best I could.

"No idea who did it?" I saw a speculative look in her eyes. I knew she suspected I did have an idea, just wasn't telling.

"No." But even as I denied it I realized I did have a suspect in mind. And absolutely no evidence to back it up.

Very un-Zoeylike, she let it go. I expected she'd circle back around to the question before I left. "Sorry I missed the last get-together of the old gang at Rocky Road. Not many still around, are there?"

"Tabi moved on to a job in Charleston. They have a facility that can give her sister better treatment. Ned finally found work and took his family to Colorado. No, not many left."

"Glad for them both. I guess I was one of the lucky ones. Thanks to your recommendation. I hope I thanked you properly for that."

"Of course, you did. As I recall you took me out to dinner, too."

She smiled. "Least I could do. What did you want to see me about?"

"I'm sure you know Marcus Oliver." I paused.

Zoey's open, friendly expression vanished in an instant. Her jaw set in a hard line. Even when she was trying to calm a belligerent Eastern employee who'd failed his drug test, I'd never seen such a look on her face.

"Yes." Her answer was clipped.

"What?"

"Actually something happened last Friday night involving him. Late."

"What." I said again.

"A fight. His face took kind of a beating. Not that I'm shedding many tears over that. He deserved it and worse."

"Has he given you trouble?"

"Tried. Have you ever met him?"

"No." I was going to have to drag it out of her. "What kind of trouble?"

I thought she wasn't going to answer. But I guess she needed someone to listen and let her talk about it in confidence. Someone she could trust. Finally she poured out the story.

"Marcus Oliver is a bigot. He's offended that the hotel employs a black woman, he didn't use that term, as head of security. You wouldn't believe what all else he said. He's a lawyer and his daddy's a powerful judge in Nashville. So the hotel is nervous about what he might do. I threatened to take them to federal court if they fired me. But I don't know how long that will keep it from happening."

I rocked back in my chair. The bastard. After what he'd done he dared throw his weight around in Wexler Bend. Not while I drew breath in this town would he cost Zoey her job.

"It just so happens I came to ask you about any possible disturbances Mr. Oliver may have been involved in here. And another man, but first Oliver. Has he made trouble for anyone, besides you, at the hotel? And what was the fight about?"

"That's what brought on my trouble. Darrell had told me Oliver was a heavy weight who thought he could get by with anything. A young girl said Oliver accosted her in the elevator at a Chamber banquet. An alderman's daughter. They didn't want the police involved, wanted me to talk to him. When I questioned him, with Darrell present, he denied it and went to the manager."

"You have recordings?" We recorded everything at Eastern for 'cover-your-ass' insurance. I'd continued doing it and I assumed Zoey did, too.

"Of course. Only reason I'm still here, I expect. They know the recording can't be used in court, since he didn't know about it, but leaks happen."

If possible my contempt for Oliver increased. He deserved to be strung up by unmentionable parts of his anatomy. Would he ever pay for his crimes? As long as his father was in a position to prevent it, I knew it was unlikely. But being a believer in the eventual triumph of good over evil, in spite of evidence to the contrary, I could hope.

"Why are you interested in what Oliver did here at the hotel? Has he done something else? Can you prove it?"

I hated to dash the hope in her sad, angry eyes. "I know he was involved in a crime in Nashville. That's why he was inflicted on Wexler Bend, more's the pity. I just have an idea, with no proof at all."

She shrugged. "Figures."

"Back to the fight. What was it about?"

"Don't know. Neither one would say. The guy who hit him was arrested, but he made bail next day. I heard yesterday the charges were dropped by Oliver. Surprised the hell out of me."

"From what you say, doesn't sound like him. His face was pretty banged up?"

"Yeah. Funny thing, though. The injuries didn't exactly look like they'd just happened."

"Really? That's odd."

"Who else was it you wanted to know about?"

What a difference from the last time I tried to find out something about a hotel guest. Zoey threatened to call the police and have me arrested. I guess she was tired of the shenanigans of the pillars of society.

"Robert Goren. One of the Veeps at Southern Moldings. I heard a rumor that he's another Nathan Taggert." I felt a twinge of guilt that I failed to mention that Taggert was now sober.

"Yeah, he does remind me of Taggert at Southern Moldings events, and other times. Oliver has no love for him either, though not for that reason."

"Oh?" I put a questioning inflection on the word. But I was pretty sure I could have guessed the reason after hearing about his reaction to Zoey.

"Mr. Goren is of Hispanic descent. Very nice, even if he can't drink responsibly. But it's the Hispanic part that bothers Oliver. Thinks the Gorens shouldn't be allowed here or at the country club. I've heard him say so."

"Figures." I repeated Zoey's cynical word. "What else do you know about the Gorens?" If Zoey was in a talkative mood, I better take advantage of it.

She thought a minute. "They brought their young daughter to a family function the company threw about four months ago. Right after Christmas. Selena's her name. The news last night said they had a tip she was the girl found dead by the river. Is it true?"

"I'm sorry to say it is. But don't repeat that until it's officially confirmed. Anything else about the party?"

She nodded and her expression grew hard again. "The parents didn't pay any attention to the girl. Dad was busy drinking himself blotto. Mom was sucking up to the mayors wife." She paused.

I waited for her to continue.

"She's – was a beautiful girl. Caught Oliver's eye. He talked to her all evening, danced with her, pulled out all the stops to charm her."

I felt pieces falling into place. It brought me no satisfaction to realize that I was right in believing Marcus

Oliver was involved in the murder of two young women. Proving it was going to be another and very difficult story, I knew.

My cell phone rang. Still looking at Zoey, I pulled it from my replacement tote bag and answered without looking at the display. "Cameron Locke."

"Formal, aren't we?"

"Oh. Mind on something else, didn't look at the phone."

"We just got a report that Robert Goren's vehicle went off the road on the edge of town and he was killed. Initial report, strong odor of alcohol. No surprise there."

"Guess Mrs. Goren will be planning a double funeral." Zoey's eyes widened. I nodded and held up a finger to indicate that I'd fill her in.

"Try and contain your sorrow, Locke." Shac's voice was dry.

"Sorry. You know how I feel about parents who don't protect their kids."

"Where are you? Nathan Taggert's trying to find you."

"He called you to locate me?"

"Go figure. He said you helped him after he got the news about Vivian. You done good, Cam."

"Thanks. I'll call him. Hate for him to crawl back in the bottle."

"Have you gone by the hospital yet?"

"No, on my way home. Dropped by to talk to Zoey. Just leaving."

"I'll come by sometime later."

"Lab find any prints on my stuff?"

"Still checking."

We clicked off and I told Zoey about Goren's accident and hugged her goodbye.

I had to sit and fidget half an hour in the Quick Care Clinic before I got to see a nurse practitioner. I watched a news channel do two repeats of the Goren accident report. The medical person pronounced that my injury was healing well. After a CNA changed the dressing I left.

I had eaten my last egg and the only food I knew I had in the fridge was a frozen Sara Lee pumpkin pie that I'd had since last Thanksgiving. I stopped at the first fast food place I came to, which was Buddy's. Not my favorite but their drive-thru was fast and the hyperactive server couldn't have cared less about my head adornment. Driving on home I wished I had also ordered a fried pie when I remembered seeing the Sara Lee box in the trash after the Task Force invasion.

Twenty-Four

I'd barely devoured my pecan chicken salad sandwich and plain fries when the glow of headlights passed across my front window. The doorbell sounded and a peephole view verified that it was Shac standing on the stone floor of the recessed entryway. His expression sent inaudible alarm bells sounding through my brain.

"What? Not somebody else dead?" Before he could answer my conscience sent a bolt of guilt through me. I hadn't yet called Nathan Taggert back.

My face must revealed how stricken I felt. "Nathan?"

"No, no. At least not that I know of."

"So why do you look like that?"

He looked at me and I knew he didn't want to tell me. I sat down. "For God's sake, just tell me."

"Goren wasn't killed by the crash."

What was he getting at? "So how did he die, then?"

"He was shot. With your gun."

I felt the blood drain from my face. Someone shot with my gun. Exactly what I'd feared when I discovered my Glock missing the morning after I'd been knocked out.

"But – the crash. How did it happen? Was someone else in the car?"

"Don't know for sure. And again, don't know for sure."

"Did the funeral home...."

"Hospital was handling several victims of a three-car pileup when he was brought in. All hands tied up so it was late before they got to Goren. Discovered the bullet hole when they were cataloging his injuries for their records. Called us. So we took another look in the car. It'd been towed by then. But your gun was in it. Slid under the seat."

"So he shot himself?"

"His fingerprints were on it. But the crime scene techs don't think he was shot in the car."

I was still trying to grasp the implications. "So that means – what exactly?"

"Very least, somebody was with him when he shot himself. Put the body in his car and staged the accident."

"Why?"

"Could have been the one who attacked you and took your gun. Wanted to get rid of it. And Goren. Maybe Goren knew him and the killer was afraid he'd tell."

"Took my gun specifically to shoot him?"

He shrugged. "Maybe."

"I never heard of Robert Goren until his daughter hired me to find her boyfriend. What's the connection?"

"Any luck in turning up the boyfriend?"

"I haven't even had time to check out the address she gave me. She said she didn't know where, or if, he worked somewhere."

"We checked the address in your notes. Empty loft above a closed second-hand store."

"So he lied to her about that. He was older, so she said, met him at the campus coffee shop."

"Didn't. No one at the coffee shop remembers seeing her there. The few friends she'd made at school, if you can call them that, more like acquaintances, said she kept to herself. Didn't know her boyfriend."

My face must have reflected my immediate idea.

"What just occurred to you?" Shac demanded.

I really needed to get better at keeping my poker face on around him. "Social media. I wonder if she had a Facebook page?"

I got up and filled our mugs with coffee, then led the way down the side hall. I sat in my desk chair to use my office computer, which had stronger encryption safeguards than the one in the house.

When I logged onto Facebook I searched for Goren, Selena and hit paydirt immediately. The youthful beauty stared out from her page, bits of cyber code and photos, if her parents had any, all that remained of that beauty. As

Shac had said, she listed only a half-dozen or so friends. Classmates from the school in Alabama, I saw, when I clicked on a couple of names. Shac wrote all the names in his notebook. Someone would have to talk to them, see if they knew anything about Selena's life after the family moved to Wexler Bend.

Unlike most girls her age, Selena had made few posts, even when she lived in Alabama. Early in January she made a single post. It included a heart that was displayed when a combination of three keys was typed. 'At last, I've found my one and only,' followed by a string of exclamation marks. One friend commented, 'who is the loser?' Selena hadn't answered.

Why, I wondered. Most attractive young girls did not lack for friends, genuine or hangers-on. Unless her father's problem with the bottle caused her to withdraw. Or...

I looked at Shac. "Did you sense any ethnic animosity when you interviewed people at the college?"

"Not overt. But then most students are fairly accepting." He thought a moment. "Unless they're bullies."

"So why did she take up with an older guy? I wonder if there was more to..."

"More to what?"

"Zoey told me – " Damn. I couldn't stop now. Would he think I was dragging Louise's law partner into this for personal reasons?

"Go on." He was adamant.

"A party just after Christmas at the Clare View. The Gorens brought Selena. And ignored her all evening. But somebody else didn't."

"Who?" Shac's face was grim. I knew he didn't understand why I was reluctant to tell him. He would in a minute.

"Marcus Oliver."

"Say what?"

"He brought her drinks, ginger ale, and danced with her. Zoey said she seemed to enjoy his attentions."

"Are you thinking he might be the mystery boyfriend?"

"It's possible. He's been involved with young girls before." I crossed my arms and prepared to stand my ground. Was he reluctant to consider Oliver because he was Louise's partner? If I played the recording of Louise's visit, I wondered if it would dilute his reluctance to consider Oliver as a possible boyfriend/suspect. Then I remembered the digital recording had been written over by now. Just as well.

When he still didn't say anything I opened my mouth to try and convince him I could be right about Marcus Oliver. And said exactly the wrong thing. "I know you think I'm just suspicious of him because he's Louise's partner. But..."

"You have no idea what I'm thinking, Cam." His voice was hard. "I'll let myself out." And before I could say another word, he was gone.

I didn't move for five minutes. Had Louise Taggert spoken the truth when she said she and Shac were now on good terms? Had he really thought I was trying to implicate Marcus Oliver to try and damage Louise's reputation?

I finally shook myself and tried to remember what it was I needed to do. Just as I remembered my phone rang and Nathan Taggert's name showed on the caller ID. I snatched it up.

"Nathan. I am so sorry I haven't gotten back to you. How are you holding up?"

"Not so good, Cam."

"Again I am so sorry. I don't have a child, but I know the pain must be almost unbearable."

"I never imagined how bad. Because I never imagined my daughter would die before me. Are you busy? If you are, please say so. I have no right to expect you to hold my hand indefinitely."

"No. I'm not. Do you want to come over?" I was tired of trying to figure out where Shac was coming from. Running the mental tape of his words over and over would not help.

"The thing is, a couple of neighbors brought over some food, a casserole and pie. I don't want to eat alone. Could I bring it over and we'd have dinner at your place?"

The request took me by surprise, but I managed to reply. "Yes. That will be fine, Nathan. In about half an hour?"

"Thank you, Cam. I'll be there."

I shut down the monitor and left my office. As I walked down the hall, I remembered that I hadn't finished telling Shac the reasons for my suspicion falling on Marcus Oliver. The other was the fact that Nathan had seen several texts from him to Vivian on her cell phone.

The texts could mean nothing, could be explained by saying he was trying to reach his partner, her mother. But Nathan had sensed something else. If Marcus was Selena's mystery boyfriend and If Vivian was involved with him, too, that meant both murdered young women had a connection with him. There had to be a way to verify if Vivian had a relationship with Oliver. The young woman at her workplace. Maybe another interview would jog her memory. If she'd ever seen them together somewhere. At work or a restaurant. It was worth a try.

I shelved the idea for the moment. I pulled dishes that hardly ever saw the light of day from cabinets, dusted off water glasses. Since fast food was my usual nourishment of choice, if you could call it that, and it came with its own serving containers my dishes were seldom called into service. Except for those needed for coffee. Someone on the Task Force, probably Jake, had loaded the dishwasher with almost all my supply of cups and mugs, and run the cycle. I somehow didn't picture Taylor Glass as the domestic type. Not that I was anymore, either.

I wondered what, if any, progress the Task Force was making. Aside from the reason for it, my head injury, I had been gratified to be included in a small part of their investigation. I really hoped they were getting somewhere.

Twenty-Five

The doorbell put punctuation to my mental questions about the Task Force. Dinner was here. When I opened the door, the raw pain in Nathan's eyes was almost too much to look upon. He held a large baking dish with a foil-covered pie on top of it. I took the pie and led the way to the seldom used, or never in my tenure, dining table. I'd even dug out some place mats that must have belonged to Dan, I didn't remember ever owning any. We uncovered the chicken and veggie casserole, which smelled heavenly, and I poured filtered water from the pitcher on the table.

He made a valiant attempt to eat, but both of us mostly pushed the food around on our plates. Even the small slices of pecan pie, one of my favorites, fared no better.

"Enough?" I finally asked. He nodded.

We left the food and dishes on the table. I'd cover it back up and let him take it home when he left. I poured more coffee and suggested we go to the living room.

Nathan sat on the floral couch and I took my easy chair. "If you want to talk…" I said.

He cleared his throat. "Captain Tawson didn't give me any details about how Vivian died. Do you know?"

I shook my head. "Not much. Just that the cause of death was a hard blow to the head from a sharp cornered something."

"So was it intentional? Accident? But why did she go to Atlanta?"

So he had not been told the nature of the person, or persons, suspected of killing Vivian. Or that she apparently had been knocked unconscious on Clare Creek Mountain prior to being bound and taken to Atlanta.

"Did she speak at all about anyone she dated, or saw regularly?" Maybe if he thought he could help find the truth about Vivian's death it would help him.

"No. They said she went to clubs, but she never mentioned her social life to me."

"Ummm. You said she had Louise's number, but did they see each other at all? Did she go to Louise's office?"

"You mean she might have met Oliver that way?"

"Yes." I drank coffee, wondering whether to pursue the subject.

"She may have. Louise gave her some expensive sandals on Thursday. It was Vivian's birthday and she'd talked us into a 'family dinner.'" He sketched quote marks in the air. "Vivian would have given them to the thrift store, but she'd been wanting those very shoes."

What did Shac say about some sandals? Or one sandal. Maybe it would come back to me.

"What brand? And did Louise know she had? Been wanting them?"

"I don't know if Louise knew. The name had something to do with food. Something sweet, maybe. Why?"

"Just batting around ideas." Even if Louise didn't know Vivian and her law partner were dating, if they were, she could have discussed what to give Vivian for her birthday with Oliver. Solicited ideas for something to make Vivian like her. Oliver could have suggested the shoes as something a young woman would like. He would know. Especially if they were in a relationship and she mentioned her wish to him.

We were lost in our own thoughts for a few minutes. The doorbell cut through the silence, startling both of us. I went to the door and opened it without checking the peephole.

Shac stood on my stone-floored entry, arms crossed over his chest. He scowled, which told me he'd guessed I'd opened the door without checking. But he walked on in without saying anything about it. He stopped when he saw Nathan sitting on the sofa.

"Taggert." He hesitated a second, glanced at me, then continued across the room, hand outstretched. Nathan rose and they shook hands.

"Sorry for your loss." Shac said.

"Thank you." Nathan looked at his watch and continued, "I'd better get on home. I'm sure you two have things to discuss."

He turned to me, saying, "Cam. Thank you. You've helped me far more than I deserve."

"Taggert." Shac held up a hand to detain him. "If you're up to answering a few questions, I'd appreciate it."

Nathan sat back down. "All right. Anything. If it'll help find the murderer of my daughter."

I went to the kitchen and brought Shac his mug filled with coffee.

He took it and said, "Thanks."

He sat on the edge of the second chair that matched the sofa, forming a conversational area in front of my gas fireplace. He looked at Nathan and asked, "Did she go up to Clare Creek Mountain Park often?"

Nathan dropped his eyes to his hands. "I don't know. But she wasn't really a nature fan. Liked clubs, shows, other inside entertainment more."

"That's our impression from what her friends have said. So, do you have any idea why she would have gone to the park on Friday?"

"The park? Was she there? Is that where she died? Then how did she get to Atlanta?"

"No, GBI is pretty certain she died in Georgia. Would her biological mother be there?"

"No. She went to New York when Vivian was ten. Vivian visited her a few times, but said she felt like she was in her mother's way."

Shac shot me a warning glance. I scowled back. Did he think I'd let my dislike of unfit parents interfere with getting information about a murder?

"Everything going okay at work? As far as you know?"

"She dropped out of school. Worked several jobs. But she seemed to have found what she wanted to do when she went to work at the dress shop."

"She wanted to stay there? Work on advancement?"

"No. Well, maybe that, too. But she was talking about enrolling at the state university, to study fashion marketing." Nathan fell silent, seeming lost in thought.

"Recently?" Shac prodded.

"At the dinner she and I had with Louise..." Nathan hesitated. I'd been wondering when this encounter would become really awkward. Both having been previously married to the same woman.

Shac did what he's so good at, ignored it. "Go on."

"A guy she was friends with made a remark about her thinness once and she decked him. She'd done a little local modeling in high school. Even though she was pretty enough to model, she was a runner, too. Later started Tae Kwon Do as a lark, and liked it. So she had a lot of confidence. But she knew twenty-one was a little late to get into professional modeling. So she looked into fashion marketing at the university. Louise didn't think marketing was a good idea. Not stable enough. Was pushing for her to choose law school."

Shac was silent for over a minute. I wondered what he was contemplating asking Nathan. If he was hesitating it must be something he dreaded bringing up. And I could pretty well guess what it was. When he finally spoke, my reading was proved correct. Though he took a different angle than I expected.

"Did you ever meet any of the people she worked with, or any other friends?"

"No. We were just getting close again. I don't think she had entirely gotten to the point of trusting me with details of her life yet." His voice broke again at the last.

"Do you know if Vivian was ever approached, maybe at one of the clubs, about working as an escort, high end type?"

Nathan jumped up, his face twisted in anger. "Absolutely not. My daughter would never be involved in something like that."

"I'm sure of it. Being approached would not be the same as considering the idea. We know people involved in that business often frequent clubs."

"Why are you asking that question?" Nathan sat down, but his hands were still fisted on his knees.

"The area where Vivian's body was found has been identified as one where human trafficking is carried on." Shac made the statement without inflection.

Nathan's hands covered his face. "Just tell me what else you know, Shac."

"I'm sorry. We believe she was abducted from Clare Creek Mountain Park. Probably knocked out. And then taken to Atlanta. Possibly to be sold into the system."

Nathan moaned. Then asked, "Because she was beautiful?"

Shac hesitated. "Yes, that. But she isn't the usual type they choose."

"Which is?"

"Younger. Feels estranged from family. Easily manipulated." He raised a hand. "I know, you said you still had problems, didn't think she trusted you yet. But she was planning for the future, school, a career. Had self-confidence."

"So why?"

"I don't know. There's something we're not getting. But we will, I promise."

"Was – was she hurt? In other ways?" Nathan's voice trembled on the last words.

"No." Shac's voice was gentle. "No. We think they didn't intend to kill her. You said she was a runner and did Tae Kwon Do. Would she have fought, attacked, given the slightest opportunity?"

"You better believe it. She didn't count the odds. My baby girl would have fought to the death."

"We think she did."

Nathan buried his face in his hands. His shoulders shook.

I walked over and stared down at the unlit gas logs in the fireplace.

In a minute Nathan asked another question. "Why take her from the park?"

"Out of the way place. Dealers in human trafficking keep low profiles." Shac's voice was more gentle than I'd ever heard it, except when he talked to me. Sometimes

"Anything you can think of might help. Will you go over everything you can remember, and I know it will be hard, but try.

"I will. But I think I'd like to go home now."

"We'll let you know what we can, when we can."

I walked him to the door, touched his arm.

Nathan looked back. "Thanks for the company, Cam. You'll never know how much I appreciate it. Will you be at the funeral?"

I nodded. Almost detained him longer. The father of one of our murder victims, Goren, had become a victim himself. Was it possible Nathan could, too? But I let him go and he drove away.

Twenty-Six

Just as I closed the door I remembered Nathan's food. "Damn."

"What?" Shac gave me a sharp look.

"I forgot to give him his leftovers."

"What leftovers?"

"His neighbors brought over some food. He didn't want to eat alone so he asked if he could bring it here. I said yes. But there's a bunch left."

"I was about to ask if you had anything to eat. Unlikely as it seemed." He picked up his mug and headed for the kitchen. He paused when he saw the dishes and food on the dining table. Gave me a look I couldn't interpret. He pulled a plate from the cabinet and piled on a generous serving of casserole and slice of pie. Refilled his mug from the Bunn and started back to the living room, plate and mug in hand.

"Didn't you have dinner with Taylor and Jake?"

"Jake went back to Georgia to check on something they found. Taylor's back in Nashville. Afraid you missed something? Or somebody?"

I refrained from taking offense. Or showing it anyway and followed him from the kitchen, after refilling my own mug. "Guess Taylor and I will have do the shooting range another time. So what do you think happened? If she was taken to be trafficked, why kill her?"

"We really don't believe it was intentional. If she regained consciousness after they brought her there, she wouldn't have submitted meekly, from what Nathan said. She was a runner. And trained in Tae Kwon Do."

"I figured, too, that she would have fought."

"Georgia lab is still working on trace." He took several bites, a swallow of coffee. "And police are still going over the area where she was dumped."

"Too bad the river probably washed away any trace evidence that might have been on Selena." I said.

Shac swallowed a last bite of pie. "Actually, it didn't. Not all of it."

"How?" I sat up straighter. He loved to keep me in suspense. At least we were back on our normal footing, it seemed.

"Because her hands were clenched from the convulsions, and remained clenched, protecting the ends of the nails, the lab found tiny bits of trace under her fingernails. She fought, too."

"Good for her," I said.

He looked down at his plate, set it on the coffee table. He opened his mouth, shut it again. He seemed to be having an internal debate, but knew he had to say something. "What were you about to tell me this afternoon?"

I hesitated a beat. But I knew it would be a cold day in a hot place if I held out for an apology. He'd probably already forgotten about his abrupt departure after I mentioned the possiblity his ex-wife's law partner could be a suspect in Selena's murder. "Zoey said Marcus Oliver was a racist. And he was involved in a fight at the hotel bar late Friday."

"Police called?"

"Yes. The other guy was arrested. Made bail next morning. And charges dropped yesterday."

"Dropped, huh?" He seemed to find that unlikely, too. Since I knew Oliver had let his friend in Nashville serve time after covering for him, I could be pretty positive that Shac, too, was aware of Oliver's history.

"Oliver taken to the hospital?"

"Not according to Zoey. Refused."

"Zoey say anything else? That might be related to these cases?"

"No."

"Wait, she told you he was a racist. What was her basis for that?"

"He tried to get the Hotel/Conference Center to let her go as Security Chief, because she's black. It happened after an alderman's daughter complained that Oliver accosted her in the elevator and Zoey questioned him about it."

"And he said that was the reason, not because she accused him?"

"Referred to her race in derogatory terms."

"Police report?"

"What do you think?"

"Okay. And?"

"And he made no secret of his feelings that the Gorens shouldn't be allowed in the hotel or the country club because of Goren's Hispanic origins." I paused. "There's one other thing."

"What?"

"Zoey said Oliver's injuries didn't look as though they'd just occurred in a fight."

"We'll try to find some witnesses. See what they say."

He got up to leave. "Head feeling okay?"

"Yes. Contractor will be here in the morning to see about installing more lights." I hesitated. "And I'm getting security cameras in and around the house."

He studied me for a moment. "Not losing your nerve, are you, Locke?"

I bristled, but inside I knew the question hit too close to home. "Of course not. Covering bases."

"Good. Better put the rest of that food in the fridge. Talk tomorrow."

"The rest? All three spoonfuls? Goodnight."

After he left I tidied up the kitchen, loaded the dishwasher and turned it on. I was happy we were back on friendly footing. What had been his problem earlier?

The next morning, Wednesday, I'd just rolled over to check the time when the phone rang. Jake Hunter's cell phone number popped up. "Good morning, Cam. Didn't wake you, did I?"

"No. But I'm barely awake. What's up?"

"I'll be heading up there later this morning. Meeting Glass at Knoxville. Can you meet us and Shac at Rocky Road at one?"

"Something new? And why not..."

"We'll talk then. Bye."

And he was gone. Didn't even give me time to ask if he'd already called Shac. And why we were meeting at Rocky Road instead of headquarters.

I showered and took advantage of the luxury of choosing which clean outfit to put on after my orgy of cleaning and laundry on Frlday. I was sipping my first cup of coffee when the doorbell rang. A man of indeterminate age, wearing a hard hat, stood on my doorstep when I looked through the peephole. When I opened the door I saw a truck with the logo of the electrical contractor I'd called. Another man was sitting in it.

The man introduced himself, produced ID, and asked where I had in mind to put the new light poles.

He declined my offer of coffee, so I took my mug and walked out to show him the corners of the yard that I wanted lit up. He pointed out that the large oak tree at the back left corner would block some of the light. So I told him to put it in front of the tree.

"Okay. We should be able to get two of the three installed today."

He asked, indicating my head. "Stumbled in the dark?"

My head had healed enough so I'd put a medium sized bandage on after my shower. I didn't want to get into telling about my attacker. "You could say that."

I told him I'd be leaving in a few minutes, would be back in the afternoon, then went back inside and left them to it.

After checking for any important emails I looked in my tote bag to make sure necessities were still in it. Wallet, notebook, pens, spare undies and tee shirt. Spare gun. Thank God, my other gun was accounted for, even if it was in an evidence locker at police headquarters. Had Rob Goren shot himself with it? Or had someone else done the deed? Either way I wasn't sure I could keep it once it was returned to me. Even though it was my favorite weapon. I still didn't have my original favorite tote bag back. Made a mental note to ask Shac about it again.

As I drove out of my driveway the men were using a huge truck-mounted borer to make a hole for one of the light poles. I'd feel a lot safer leaving and returning to my house at night after the lights were installed.

My destination was *Vicki's on Lyn*, to talk to Vivian's thin to the point of emaciation co-worker.

Twenty-Seven

I was glad no other customers were in the store when I walked in. Probably Manager Zarnes was not as pleased. I was also glad he was not in sight.

"Hello, Yvonne, remember me?"

"Have you found Vivian yet?"

Not a news junkie, I guessed. "I'm sorry to say, her body was found in Georgia. She'd been killed."

"How awful. I wonder if Mr. Zarnes knows?" An odd question since I was pretty sure she and Mr. Zarnes were 'close,' the euphemism usually employed for such liaisons.

"Maybe you can tell me something I didn't ask you the other day."

"If I can."

"Did Vivian have a boyfriend, that you know of."

"She had been seeing someone. But she didn't tell me his name. She seemed a little secretive about him."

"So you never saw him."

"Not to see his face. I was passing by the shop as she was leaving on one of my days off once and saw him pick her up."

"But not him? What did you see?"

"His hot car. An expensive sports car. Must have cost a bundle."

"Did you recognize the model? What color?"

"Shiny black. Must have just had it detailed. No." She shook her head. "I don't know the different models. But it didn't have a back seat."

So, a smaller sports car. I'd looked up Oliver's vehicle. A single seat Jaguar. Black.

I asked a few more questions, but Yvonne had told me all she knew. As I walked to my car I noticed Zarnes walking rapidly toward his store. A smear of bright red on the corner of his mouth caught my eye. I wondered how Yvonne would react to it.

Slowly I was accumulating more reasons to suspect that Marcus Oliver had killed, or at least been involved in, the killing of two young women. Evidently he could charm women of any age. I sincerely hoped we would not find other victims of his monstrous activities. Was he working alone? With his money he could hire any number of low lifes to assist him.

I remembered that I hadn't checked the finances of the Olivers, father and son. Not that I'd find out much about the elder Oliver's probably. They would be more heavily safeguarded from prying eyes.

I checked my watch. Still an hour or so before I had to leave to meet the guys at Rocky Road. I could go by the funeral home and sign the book for Selena Goren. I'd promised Nathan I would attend Vivian's funeral tomorrow. But Selena's memorial service was at the same time I'd be meeting Shac, Jake, and Taylor. The funeral was postponed and would be a double funeral when Rob Goren's body was released. In spite of all I'd heard about her, I felt a twinge of sympathy for Alva Goren. Even she must be going through a terrible time.

Thankfully no one was around when I stepped into the funeral home foyer or the hallway outside the room where Selena's service was scheduled. I tried to avoid looking as I passed the doorway, but I glimpsed a few flower arrangements including the one I'd ordered, red Canna lilies. I'd also ordered one for Vivian. A large and ornate one in the center of the small semi-circle must be the family flowers. An open visitors book lay on a chest high stand near the doorway. Only two lines held writing. I grabbed the pen and quickly scrawled my name on the third line. Below the only other name were the words, 'Southern Moldings, CFO.' Figured.

I left the funeral home with relief and headed toward Rocky Road Sports Bar. I was a few minutes early, but Jake and Taylor were waiting. Rhonda, the black-haired, forty-something hostess, asked if we were ready to be seated when I joined them. Jake looked at Taylor and me and we nodded. "Sure. Our other buddy should be along in a few minutes."

"I'll bring Sergeant Lane to the table as soon as he arrives." Rhonda said.

Jake looked surprised and Taylor mirrored his expression.

"Small town," I said, when we were seated and Rhonda walked away. "She seated us when we were here last."

Jake still stared at Rhonda's retreating back. "But that was last year. And it was Louise, not Taylor, with us."

"Shac's ex?" Taylor raised her perfectly sculpted eyebrows. "What else have I missed?"

I explained to both of them. "Rhonda forgets no one. Even if you were not so striking, Taylor, you could come back a year from now, or two or five, and she'd remember you. And that you were with us."

"Eidetic memory, huh?" Taylor asked.

I shrugged. "I guess. She's always done it."

"And working as a hostess in a restaurant." She shook her head.

I didn't tell her Rhonda owned the place. She was the big-shot TBI agent, let her discover it on her own. I was being petty, probably a result of my just realized thought that lately Shac, and Jake, were spending more time with her than me.

Our server asked for our drink orders, wrote them on her pad. "Wasn't eavesdropping. We use Rhonda's memory all the time. Like to tell us where our customer with a certain earring is sitting when we forget. I don't know what we'd do without her."

"Interesting." Taylor said.

"Thanks, uh, Wanda," Jake said, after he checked her nametag.

Just then Shac arrived at the table. "See you on the way out, Rhonda. I'll leave my check for you."

"Right," she laughed. "Hope springs eternal, Sarge."

I knew what she meant, but waited for one of the others to ask. Jake did. Shac said, "Tell 'em, Cam. I want to look at the menu."

Even without an eidetic memory, as far as I knew anyway, Shac had memorized the menu long ago. But I explained. "He and Rhonda have a running bet. If he can tell who was sitting at the five nearest tables all during his meal she'll pay his tab."

Wanda brought our drinks, iced tea all around. So the three LEOs must be on duty, and took our orders. The nearest wall television was on, loud enough so we probably wouldn't be overheard, but we could talk comfortably enough.

Jake and Taylor looked at Shac. I set my glass down. "Okay. Why have I been included in what appears to be a working lunch for you three?"

Shac stared into his glass. The others waited. He finally spoke. "When you returned from Georgia Saturday night and Mears took you to the station, he handled your tote bag, right?"

"He asked me to hand it to him. I was surprised, to put it mildly, but gave it to him and he kept it until we left the station and he took me back home. He did apologize."

"Did he look into the bag, pull your gun, anything else, out."

"No, not that I saw."

"Was he out of your sight at any time while in possession of your bag, Cam?" His eyes were hard, but I knew him well enough to see a trace of pain behind the hardness.

I closed my eyes and thought back to Saturday "No. He wasn't."

"So he didn't handle the contents of your bag at all, as far as you know?"

"No." I didn't like the implications his questions were raising in my mind. "Shac. Why?"

"The techs finished fingerprinting everything in your bag. They found prints belonging to Mears on several items."

None of us said anything for a minute. Taylor and Jake didn't seem surprised, so I guessed they already knew.

"Well, I guess it's possible he touched some things while I was talking to Captain Tawson. He still had my bag. But why would he?"

"Including the case with your, uh, personal stuff under your extra clothes? And the compact mirror, also on the bottom? Rummaging in your bag right in front of Tawson?"

I didn't want to hear this. I liked Don. And now I understood the pain in Shac's eyes.

I asked, in a very quiet voice, "So what are you saying, Shac? Don's the person who knocked me out Monday night, emptied my bag and took my gun?"

"Maybe. We think the gun was a 'just in case it was needed' for some CYA."

"And a police detective failed to remember he was leaving fingerprints on my stuff?"

"Maybe because he was in a hurry. The main reason for your attack was probably to look for something in your files about Selena's case. Something that might lead to her killer. Remember she wasn't killed on purpose. So no advance planning."

"And there was very little time to search because whoever it was couldn't shut off the alarm," I said.

"Plus he probably never expected his fingerprints to come into play. And I told you a little more of a direct blow to your temple and you'd have been dead. Mears would have known how and where to strike so as not to kill."

I still wasn't convinced and I guess my doubts showed.

"Back to Saturday. You said you almost wrecked on your way home."

I looked at him. "You can't think that was deliberate. Dozens of people could have been killed. And Don would have been with -" I stopped. "You were on your way to Alabama."

"He was off for the weekend, too much OT. But he called Captain Tawson, asked if there was any news on the girl. She'd been identified, the car found, your receipt."

"So he was in town, not on I-75 at Chattanooga, trying to kill me and a bunch of others."

"He called again, later in the afternoon. An hour or so before you got home. I'd told Tawson about when you'd arrive. Mears offered to bring you to the station."

"And again, what motive would he have had to attack me on Monday?"

Instead of answering he asked another question. "Do you know what Don's personal vehicle is?"

"No. What is it?"

He tapped keys on his phone and turned it toward me. On the screen was a photo of the two of them leaning against an unremarkable pickup truck. A pickup with very dark tinted windows. My blood chilled. It could have been the pickup that almost forced me into the path of a speeding eighteen-wheeler.

Without my permission my brain started figuring scenarios if it had been Don on I-75. My death in a multi-car Interstate pileup would need no explanation. But if I was dead in my own driveway it would.

We stopped talking when Wanda appeared with our food. She refilled tea glasses, asked if we needed anything else.

Twenty-Eight

I wasn't ready to sign off on Don Mears as my attacker just yet. At the risk of raising Shac's ire, I asked, "Do we know where Marcus Oliver was during the relevant times?"

"According to Zoey, getting into a fight at the Clare View on Friday night. By your own report." Shac replied, without expression. "Not seen on Saturday by anyone we've talked to until dinner at the Clare View, drinking late in the bar again."

"Has anyone talked to the other guy involved in the fight Friday night?"

He nodded. "Taylor did."

"You?" I turned to her. "How did you explain Task Force involvement?"

"I was back in Nashville, where he'd gone Saturday after making bail. I did tell him I was part of the Task Force, just asking some routine questions about the fight on behalf of Wexler Bend PD. He'd already scored with the money Oliver gave him. He didn't want to go to prison like the last friend who aided and abetted Oliver. Afraid to be dried out cold turkey."

"So what was the fight about?" I asked.

"No real fight. Oliver paid him to pretend to hurt him, to explain the marks on his face."

"Did he say why Oliver needed the marks explained?"

She turned a hand sideways. "Said he didn't ask. Just wanted the money."

Shac explained. "We believe Vivian landed at least one punch, offensive, not defensive. Broken bones in both hands, as though they were clasped together. Either when they were tied or as a martial arts move."

Jake took up the story. "We haven't been able to place him in Georgia. Still looking."

"And no grounds for a court order for DNA, more's the pity," Taylor said.

"A shuttle driver does remember Vivian riding up to the park Friday morning. But we already knew she'd been there from the rose in her pocket."

"Aren't there security cameras in the park now?" I asked.

Shac answered. "A bunch of them. We've had people going over the video files since Monday night when we got access, takes time."

Wanda passed our table with an armload of dirty dishes. "Something wrong with the food, folks?"

I looked at our plates. We had hardly touched our food. Jake gave her a warm smile. "No, Wanda. It's great, as usual. We've just been talking."

She smiled, deep dimples showing. She shook her white-blonde bangs back and headed on toward the kitchen.

Shac took a few bites of barbecue ribs. I moved my home fries around my plate. To be threatened and almost killed by someone who hates you is one thing. For someone you've considered a friend to want you dead is something else. To have to suspect his partner of wanting your girlfriend – I brought that line of thought to a halt in a hurry. Who said Shac considered me his girlfriend? Certainly he'd never said it. Never mind that kiss on top of the head as we left the parking garage in Roswell. That was just a friendly buddy buss.

"But – why take..." My voice trailed away as I tried to get my mind back on the subject at hand. Whether or not Don Mears wanted me dead. And if so, why?

"Your gun?" Shac asked. "We're guessing just in case he had to shoot somebody, maybe. Wouldn't do to use his own weapon."

"Guess. Just in case. If he did knock me out, I'd really like to know the reason."

"Yeah, me, too." Shac drank some tea. He clearly didn't want to keep tallying the evidence that his partner was the culprit. But he forged on. "Tawson found an indication, of sorts. Mears is living on borrowed money. And the kind of lenders he's into don't take kindly to losing their principal or interest."

So two people involved in the case were living beyond their means. In debt. Did they know each other? How?

We finished lunch and paid, Shac having to pay his own tab again, and went our separate ways. I got in my car, still trying to come to terms with the idea that Don Mears had attacked me.

The Task Force had been searching the river bank for days, trying to find the place Selena had gone into the water. Their numbers were augmented by as many bodies as local municipal and county police departments could spare. A couple of dogs had been brought in late Saturday and Sunday, but had no success either. Shac said they were reluctant to enlist many volunteers, with no idea what locals could be involved. He and Mears had helped on Monday. As we now suspected, Don had an ulterior motive. He'd volunteered in order to keep an eye on what was discovered. In case they found where the girl died. Was he the killer? I could not wrap my head around that possibility.

Such a horrible way for a young girl to die, with her whole life before her. Had she gotten into drug transport for the money? Or another reason? Was she aware of her family's financial problems? Had either parent been involved, used their daughter in such a despicable way?

I drove out Branch Drive, for lack of any specific idea of where to look that hadn't been covered. Branch Drive narrowed to two lanes a couple of miles out of town, then meandered its curvy route through the countryside at the base of Clare Creek Mountain. I passed a fairly new service station/convenience store. A half-mile or so further on, the road crossed Clare Creek, now at normal levels instead of almost overflowing as it had been for several days after a week of rain. I didn't see any people in the undergrowth along the stream. The searchers hadn't reached this area, apparently. Further downstream in some places the creek banks were overgrown with bushes and even small trees. Not likely her body had been discarded in those areas, but there were trails so they had to be checked.

Twenty-Nine

Rounding another curve I came upon Longhollow Condos. Where Selena's car had been found on Saturday. And she'd been identified by the registration and I became involved by the receipt found in the car. I pulled into a parking space to consider those facts and where they might lead.

I had been there for several minutes, absently tapping my knuckles on the steering wheel, when someone knocked on my driver side window. I lowered it. An older woman in jogging clothes stood there, holding a cane with a dog's face carved on the end of it.

"Hello, ma'am." I gave her a sunny, at least I tried for that, smile.

"Are you waiting for someone, young lady?" Her voice was business-like, not exactly hostile, but close. The message was clear. If I wasn't waiting for someone, I'd better move along.

"Umm. No. I was just thinking about something. Didn't mean to trespass."

"This is private property." She pointed the cane toward the sign that said so.

"I'm a private investigator." I pulled out my license and showed it to her. "You know about the car found here Saturday belonging to a young girl who was killed, I expect."

"A terrible thing. We're all on edge. To think the killer may have been right here on the grounds." She was quite willing for me to tarry so she could vent indignation on the nerve of a killer to transgress the grounds of their condo complex.

"Yes, ma'am. It is terrible. Did you see the car yourself?"

"No!" The negative rang out strongly. Probably wished she had been home. "I was gone to visit my son in Knoxville when the police were swarming around after they found it. And to think that girl transported drugs in it. Maybe she left it here."

I didn't explain that the police were sure the killer had left it and been picked up by someone. A resident? I made a mental note to ask Shac if all the residents had been cleared. "Do you think anyone else may have seen the car while it was here? Know how long it sat in the parking lot?"

She shook her head, with some regret, I thought. "The police questioned everyone. No one admitted noticing it. Everyone's oblivious, these days."

Certainly not her, I figured. But the car was left presumably on Wednesday night. "When did you leave for Knoxville?"

"Thursday morning. If I'd been home that car would have been found sooner."

No doubt. I really wished the old biddy had been home. "Thanks, have a good day, ma'am."

I waited until she was well up the driveway from my car before backing out of the parking space and driving out the driveway to the county road.

I'd noticed the variety of luxury cars in the parking areas. The Infiniti had fit right in so no one paid attention to it.

I drove on past the Longhollow complex for a mile or so, thinking. If the killer left the car at the complex, and everyone assumed he had, maybe he had killed Selena not far from there. He wouldn't have wanted to drive too far for fear of someone seeing and remembering the Infiniti. Longhollow was maybe two miles from the river, or creek, as it was now, with the water level back to normal. On impulse I backed into a wide area in front of a wire gate leading into a pasture. Made a three point turn and headed back toward Longhollow and the creek.

After passing Longhollow I slowed to a crawl, scrutinizing the sides of the road. A few long driveways led down through meadows toward a couple of rambling houses and some more ornate and modern McMansion types. I crossed the bridge, still searching. And found it. Or at least a lane which led off to the right a hundred feet or so past the bridge. It hardly looked used at all. I started to turn in, then changed my mind. If the killer had driven down that lane and back out, I didn't want to obliterate any indications of it.

So I drove on up Branch Drive, just past the lane, and pulled as far off the shoulder as possible. I looked at my footwear. My oldest pair of sneakers. Maybe I'd had a premonition. I checked for traffic and got out with my tote bag and stepped off the road. Weeds and brush impeded my progress as I walked parallel to the lane. Only fifty feet or so away from the road, I could look past the lane and see the moving stream of water occasionally through a break in the bushes along the bank.

About a quarter mile in, I saw that the lane ended in a cleared area, dirt showing through grass and small bushes that had not yet completely taken over. And even from where I stood, I saw tire marks. Suddenly I felt uneasy. Looked around. Suppose the killer had been here, might he return to the scene of the crime? I could hardly believe so, but criminals do strange things.

I pulled out my cell phone and dialed Shac's number. No answer. So I called Dispatch.

I gave my name and asked her to contact Shac on the police radio and tell him I had some information for him. And ask him to meet me on Branch Drive, right before the bridge. She said she would immediately. Just before I disconnected I heard her begin the call. A misgiving hit me and I could have kicked myself. I didn't really believe Don Mears had tried to kill me? Did I? If he and Shac were not together and he heard the call, he might show up. And what? Dispatch and everyone who heard the call knew my location. He wouldn't try anything. Would he? Even if he was not what I wanted to believe.

I fidgeted while I waited, afraid to move around much. Never mind if my hunch turned out to be right, I was probably already slated for a chewing out. From Shac if not Tawson. Several cars had passed on Branch Drive while I stood there. I hoped no one scraped my car. Another eased along the road, I could see the light rack moving above the tall weeds. I tensed and stepped behind a tree.

The light rack stopped moving, just past my car I thought. I couldn't actually see my car. Shac's Kia didn't have a light rack. Maybe a routine patrol. The car suddenly took off and I lost sight of it. A minute later I heard the sound of a moving car on the road again. Then it stopped and the engine shut off. Had the patrol car come back? Maybe not, I couldn't see a light rack.

The car didn't turn into the lane. At least if it was Shac who had arrived he had read the situation. I'd forgotten to have Dispatch tell him to park near my car. I peeked around the tree trunk. Somebody was moving through the weeds. The person got within a couple hundred yards and I let out the breath I didn't realize I'd been holding when I recognized Shac. I heaved a sigh of relief and stepped away from the tree.

He saw me. "Cam. What do you have?"

"Don't know for sure. Glad you're a quick study though. I forgot to tell her to tell you – "

He interrupted, "Always said we make a good team."

"Did another officer come by here earlier, do you know?"

"Don't know. I can try to find out. Why?"

"Thought I saw a squad car move by slowly, stop briefly, but moved on."

He walked closer to where I stood, looked over the weeds at the lane. His eyes narrowed. "Talk to me. How'd you wind up here after we left Rocky Road?"

"Came to the intersection with Branch, turned on it. Just drove for a ways. Came to Longhollow Condos."

"Where her car was found." He kept scanning the area between us and the creek. "Tire tracks. Have to hand it to you, Locke."

He pulled out his phone and punched a speed dial key. After a second I heard two voices answer but couldn't distinguish whose they were.

"Better get out here to the creek, just off Branch Drive. Bring all the troops and equipment. Park along the road where Cam and I are parked. We'll need a wide perimeter."

"Task Force?" I asked.

"Yeah. Taylor and Jake should be here in ten minutes."

"You think it really is something? Maybe where she was killed?"

He looked at me. "So do you. You knew when you saw the lane."

I had known. Had Selena guided me to the place she died? Who knew? I just wanted the monster who caused her death found and put away. He hadn't even tried to get help. Although from things I'd read, even if she'd been in the best ER in the country when it happened, they couldn't have saved her.

Thirty

In a few minutes the troops started arriving. They parked on the road as instructed. They all walked in through the weeds, waited for Jake's and Taylor's orders. And stood around until casts had been made of all tire tracks, in and out, by the technicians. Then other technicians swarmed, all taking pains to keep to the same paths.

In only a few minutes Taylor came over to where Shac and I stood holding up a tree. "This is it. We found where she vomited. Ground still showing disturbance from her convulsions. Drag marks to the creek."

I bit the inside of my lip. Only hours after she'd left me, she lay dead in the dirt of this deserted area. And no convenient surveillance cameras to record her killer's actions. Of course, so far none had been found on the park's cameras either. But there was a lot of video to go through. There was a good chance it was there.

Jake joined us under the tree. "Dark soon. We'll have to call it a day. And post guards. All this activity has attracted a sizable group of sightseers. And reporters."

"We could hold a short press conference, give them something." Taylor said. "Maybe at that convenience store up the road. Plenty of light there."

"Okay." Jake nodded.

"Your call." Shac said.

We made our way back to the road and our vehicles. After standing so long I was happy to sit in my car while uniformed cops cleared a way for us to leave. We parked near the rear on the side of the store away from the pumps. I started toward the spot where Taylor was already supervising the setup for the press conference in front. The building was painted a light color all over. I guess I had cameras on the brain. I'd been kicking around the idea of cameras around my house. I noticed them, the Infrared variety, on each corner of the store. I saw Shac and worked my way around to him. A good number of spectators had already followed us.

I didn't see Jake and asked where he was. Shac jerked his head toward the store. "Inside. Trying to explain to the clerk what's going on. Lady doesn't have a real good command of English. Taylor may have to go in."

I raised my eyebrows. "Why? Surely Jake can handle it."

"She speaks half-a-dozen languages."

"Oh." Clearly there was a lot more to Taylor Glass than I knew. How had she acquired half-a-dozen languages?

As usual Shac read my mind. "Couple in college. Stint with Vista. Then next five years as a combination liaison/security agent with the State Department. She was stationed in some Godforsaken country, kidnapped and taken to the desert with a wounded Attache from the compound. Saved his life when she killed the kidnappers and flew the chopper back to the Consulate. Reprimanded because her gun wasn't authorized. Decided to chuck the Feds and go into law enforcement at the state level."

"And the rest, as they say, is history." I said.

"She admires you."

I shot a look up at him to see if he was joking. Didn't seem to be. Taylor Glass admired me? For the life of me I couldn't imagine why.

Just then a burst of static sounded through a loudspeaker, then Taylor's voice as she began speaking.

"Folks, I am Taylor Glass, Special Agent with the Tennessee Bureau of Investigation and member of the Joint Southeastern Special Task Force. We want to let you know a little about what's going on just down the road here. The Joint Task Force, in cooperation with local police, has determined that the area we are checking out was connected with the recent deaths of one of two young women. Active investigation of the site will probably be ongoing for several days. We are asking the public to avoid the site so as not to contaminate any evidence and complicate a future case against the perpetrator.

"If anyone has questions, I'll answer a few now."

Instantly the several representatives of local media threw questions at her. I recognized the local 'watchdog' of the television station in a nearby town. Even the anchor had showed up, cameraman in tow. Cynically, I was sure what drew their attention was that one of the victims was the stepdaughter of a high profile local attorney. They'd really go into a frenzy if they knew the only suspects at the moment were a police detective and a prominent local resident who happened to be the son of a leading jurist in the state capital.

In a few minutes Taylor skillfully wrapped the impromptu press conference up and agents began dismantling the makeshift podium.

We started back to our cars. I paused to look up at the cameras. Shac kept walking. After a couple of steps, when he realized I wasn't beside him, he stopped. "What is it, Locke?"

I glanced down the road at the glow of lights where police and technicians still worked at the crime scene. "There are only tire tracks of one car, in and out, down there. Either they came all the way from town together, or met somewhere and then went to the river."

He nodded. "Go on."

"This would be a convenient place to meet. Then go down there for more privacy, to talk or…"

"Retrieve the drugs," he finished. "He sure didn't intend to kill her. Certainly not until the drugs were out of her."

I indicated the cameras mounted at each corner of the building. "Is there enough probability they met here to make it worth looking at a bunch more video recordings?"

"If they're available, probably so. I'll run it by Taylor."

"Run what by me?" Taylor caught up with us, evidently having heard what Shac said.

Just then I saw the rental car Jake was driving pull out of the parking area. "There goes your ride, Taylor."

"Jake has something he needs to go check on. I wondered if I could bum a ride to town with one of you. I need to coordinate with Captain Tawson."

"Sure." Shac said. "Cam saw all the cameras on this building. And thought there might be a possibility that Selena didn't drive to the scene with her killer, but could have met him here."

Taylor made a face. "And starred in some more video, which we'll need to plow through gigabytes of, to verify. Or not."

"Pretty much."

She shrugged. "But there's probability enough. We'd better do it. Any chance that you'd volunteer another pair of eyes, Cam?"

"If it might help catch Selena's killer? You bet."

And if it turned out to be Marcus Oliver, I'd be doubly vindicated. Not that that was the reason I wanted to help. I wanted whoever had destroyed that young woman to pay for it.

Taylor went inside to get the information on the company providing security for the convenience store/service station. When she returned she said she'd contact me when the footage from the cameras became available and I could come down to the station to begin searching.

Shac and Taylor left for headquarters to fill in Captain Tawson on the crime scene information. I stopped by Buddy's on my way home to pick up a sandwich, since Shac had pretty well finished off the chicken casserole from Nathan Taggert's neighbor.

Thirty-One

Since it was after working hours the electrical contracting crew was not around. But I had two new halogen security lights casting illumination nearly all around my house. Once inside I went to pour myself a mug of coffee. Ken, the installer from my own security company, had left a note on the counter.

"Ms. Locke, I'm sure you know about the video surveillance in your office since it is part of your computer system. Did you know the previous owner had begun installing security cameras connected to that system through all the rest of the house? Some of the wiring had been completed. We checked it out, then continued the installation. I hope it's okay with you for us to do it that way. The living room, kitchen and hallway are covered. We installed a temporary control station in the entertainment center cabinet in your bedroom as you instructed. It is also connected to the office system. We'll be back out tomorrow to finish up."

Dan had indeed been a security nut. But he'd never mentioned the video security he was having installed in the house. Why was he doing it? And why hadn't he told me or mentioned it in his letter to me, in which I'd learned he'd left me the house? I carried my coffee and sandwich to the bedroom to check out the control station. On the way I made note of the locations of the cameras. They were well camouflaged, blended in with the wallpaper and architectural details, molding, et cetera. If I hadn't known what I was looking for I wouldn't have noticed them.

Ken had left instructions in an envelope inside the cabinet. I scanned them and clicked the remote. Five pictures sprang to life on the upper half of the large monitor screen inside the cabinet. Three were from inside my living area and the fourth and fifth were views of my office. When Ken finished there would be six. The sixth would be the guest bedroom, toggled between it and the guest bathroom and between my bedroom and bathroom. I'd debated the cameras in the bathrooms. But burglars and/or other perpetrators do sometimes hide in bathrooms. There was a secret disconnect for those cameras. I hoped that I would remember to use it if the need arose for privacy in those areas.

The lower half of the screen would give views of the outside, now well lit by my new lights. Only the front door camera was active at the moment. I might go broke paying my electric bill, but I could feel safer until then.

After checking out the system I went on to my office to finish my dinner and check email for potential clients. My antivirus protection program informed me that an attempt had been made to access my system, but it had been thwarted. The program also gave me the IP address from which the attempt had been made.

The information not included might as well have said, 'Your problem now, baby.'

I tried my usual trace attempts, but had no success. I tried one more avenue and a message in large white letters jumped out at me. "Are you afraid of the dark?" The web address in the address bar looked like gibberish to me. This looked like a search that was beyond my skills and I might be advised to back out of it. I closed the page and decided I'd let the guy that I called on when I was stumped try to trace the hacker.

What could this weird hacking attempt have to do with the murder of the two young women? If it did. And the attack on myself in my own yard. Although my connection with the second victim, Vivian Taggert, was only after the fact. And not forgetting Robert Goren. What was the connection between his death and the murder of his daughter and Vivian? Simply what it seemed? Sorrow and guilt because he felt responsible somehow for Selena's death? How had my gun come into his possession? Or was it in a killer's possession. Was the killer the one who knocked me out and stole my gun? Was it Don Mears? How was Goren connected to him? And why had the killer, be it Don or Oliver or someone else, given it to him? So many questions and so few answers.

I was fairly certain Goren was not the assailant who knocked me out in my driveway. A person who drinks a lot reeks of alcohol. Someone who neither smokes nor drinks is especially sensitive to the odor. And I had not detected an odor of alcohol just prior to being hit.

The front doorbell rang as I entered the bedroom after my shower. I looked at the camera giving a view of the front entrance. Don Mears. What did he want? And how could I act normal toward him knowing what we suspected. The bell rang again. Needed to do something, he had to know I was home, my car was in the driveway.

I wrapped a towel around my head, belted my robe and stopped in the bedroom to put my gun in the pocket. Could I shoot Don? I thought I could, if I felt threatened.

I opened the door but left the storm door closed and locked. "Don, what can I do for you?"

He grinned. "Just checking on you. I saw Shac down at the station before I went off duty. He said you were fine, but I wanted to see for myself."

"That's nice of you. But I've just showered. Need to dry my hair and get ready for bed."

"Turning in early, huh?"

"Been a long day."

"Yeah. Scuttlebutt at the station is you found the crime scene where the girl died. Good for you."

"Thanks. Lucky, I guess."

"Not just luck. Well, I won't keep you. Good night, Cam." He touched his temple in a friendly salute and turned to go. He turned back. "By the way, have you come up with anything that might help identify the person who hit you?"

I shook my head, I hoped it looked regretful. "I wish. Good night, Don."

"You got new lights, didn't you?" He gestured toward the back.

I laughed. "Yeah, I do get some smarts now and then, even if it does take a knock on the head."

I wanted to bite my tongue as soon as the words were out. Did my face change? Thank God, he did leave then. I didn't know how much longer I could have kept up the charade.

I closed the door and reset the alarm code. Which I still hadn't given to Shac. Too much else going on.

My phone rang. So much for getting to bed early. It was Shac.

"We did a more thorough look at Mears's financials. Seems he's been visiting the offsite gambling parlor across the state line since it opened. Credit cards maxed out, a good-size loan outstanding, even borrowed against his 401K. Guess that truck isn't just a personal statement. He can't afford something better."

"Shac."

"What?"

"He was just here."

"There? Did you let him in?"

"No. I'd just got out of the shower. Told him I was going to bed."

"Gone now?"

"Yes. At least he drove away."

"Your lights are working, right?"

"Yes. And some of the outside cameras."

"Did he notice them?"

"No. But he mentioned the lights. I guess he remembered from bringing me home Saturday that it was darker."

"Or from when he conked you on the head Monday night."

"Oh, and somebody tried to hack into my computers."

"Succeed?"

"Not according to the security program. But I haven't been able to find out where it came from."

"Our guy'll check, if you want."

"Maybe. I'll see."

Thirty-Two

Next morning the electricians and Ken arrived again as I was leaving for police headquarteers. I assured him that what he had done yesterday was fine and I appreciated the good work.

Taylor had called to say they had received the footage from the service station. A couple of techs were reviewing it, but I could come down and help any time. Shac grabbed me before I reached the squad room where the techs were searching the security footage. "Come on."

"Where?"

"Talk to a neighbor of Mears."

"Why?"

"She called in Tuesday to report someone skulking around. Called 911, then called back a few minutes later to say it was okay, a policeman had been looking for his dog. The operator had already closed the report."

"Was it Mears?"

"That's what we're going to find out. I hope. The name was dropped from the report."

"Does Don have a dog?"

"Nope."

Since he was not forthcoming with information, I tried to figure some things out myself. For one, why had Don Mears come by my house last night? Fishing expedition? To see if I remembered anything that pointed to him as being my assailant? If I had, and he picked up on it, what would he have done? I really didn't want to think about that. If he was involved, was he Selena's killer? Or Marcus Oliver?

Shac interrupted my churning thoughts. "Do you know Maxie Filner?"

"What's she got to do with the case?"

"Do you?"

"Yes. Since you're asking, you must know that she was head accountant at Eastern Fabricators when I worked there. And still works for Southern Moldings."

"Did you know she dated Don Mears?"

I jerked my head around to look at him. "No. Do they still? Date?"

"Don't know. We'll go see her after talking to the neighbor."

I had mixed feelings about visiting Southern Moldings. I hadn't been back since I was given my walking papers. I had no reason to visit the place. Maxie was one of only a few people I used to know who still worked there.

I saw that we had reached Don's neighborhood. I'd never been there though I'd known generally where he lived. It was a nice enough working class subdivision near the edge of town. It's nicest features were that it was built on a few low, wooded hills. Don's house sat on one of the hills, trees on the left side and back, now almost fully leafed out in their new spring green. Shac drove on, turned the corner, and drove past three houses before he stopped at a white house with blue shutters sheltered by trees on three sides. Must keep the house dim inside, I thought.

"Notice anything about the location?"

"Just behind this subdivision is the road where Goren's car went down an embankment." I replied.

He nodded. We got out and started up the neat sidewalk lined with spring flowering plants to the door of the white house. Before we reached the door it opened and an older woman with short, curly gray hair stood inside the screen door.

"Can I help you? I don't need anything and I'm happy with my church."

I smothered a smile as Shac pulled out his detective shield folder. "I'm Sergeant Shackleford Lane, and this is Detective Locke. Are you Mrs. Klausner?"

I hoped she didn't notice me lift an eyebrow before I could prevent it. Of course, he had to identify me some way. And some people don't care for private detectives.

She peered intently at the folder, then at his face. "I am. I called for the police two days ago, but I called back to say I was sorry to bother you when it was a policeman I saw."

"Yes, ma'am. We appreciate that. This is just a routine follow up. May we come in?"

"Well, sure."

She opened the door and we filed past her into a living room crowded with furniture and bric-a-brac on every flat surface. Framed photographs, tiny statuettes of angels, Tiny Cherub figurines, decorative bowls. I noticed one unusual object, not your usual decorative trifle, a small pair of binoculars.

She indicated we should sit on the sofa, which was so filled with plump pillows there was hardly room to sit. "Ask your questions, Detective Lane. I didn't expect a police visit when it was just my nervousness showing."

"Always call us when you have any concerns, Mrs. Klausner. It's our job to check out anything that worries you."

"Thank you, Detective. It's good to know you don't mind."

"Now, why don't you tell us exactly what happened two days ago that concerned you."

"Well, I was standing at my kitchen sink, washing vegetables for supper. I saw this figure moving in sort of a stealthy way through the woods in the back. I could just make out that it was a man."

"Did he see you?" Shac asked.

"I stepped back, but just as I did, he looked toward me. My kitchen light was on, so I'm sure he did see me."

"What did you do then?"

"Why, I grabbed my cordless phone from the counter and dialed 911. When she answered I told her a man was skulking around my house. She said to stay put and she'd send someone out. Just then there was a knock on my kitchen door. I could see it was him. I told the 911 operator and she said not to open the door. So I didn't."

"Did he at any time make any threatening motions?"

"Oh, no. He was smiling. After the operator said it was okay to open the door, he said I was smart to 'call it in.'" Her voice put quotes around the last three words.

"So how did you know the man was a policeman?"

The house was small and the living room and kitchen opened into each other. She pointed toward her kitchen door, clearly visible. "As you see, there's glass in my door. And the storm door, too. He held a folder like yours up to the glass, with a badge and all. I was scared, but I walked over and looked at it. I told the operator the name and badge number on it. She asked if he looked like the picture and I said 'yes.' She said he was a policeman who lived nearby. As it turned out, he just lives a few houses from here. He guessed who I was talking to. He called through the glass to let him talk to her. I opened the inside door, but not the storm door, and I held the phone up to the glass. He told her who he was, the same name as on the ID. When I talked to her again, she said it was okay. So I let him in."

"And he said he was walking in the woods because -?" Shac asked at the end of her recitation.

"He was looking for his dog. It had escaped from his yard. He didn't want it to bother the neighbors. He said he was sorry to have frightened me."

"And then he left?"

"I offered him a cup of tea, but he thanked me, said no, he needed to find his dog before it got him into trouble."

"He went on home then?"

"Actually he went back into the woods, whistling and calling for the dog."

I was curious. "What name did he call the dog, Mrs.Klausner?"

She said. "I believe it was 'Marco.'"

Shac asked her a few more questions about the time of day when she saw the policeman, did she see him again. Or since. She hadn't and asked if we knew him. Shac said yes, we did, but did not elaborate.

Shac started to rise, then looked at Mrs. Klausner. "One more thing, Ma'am. I believe the policeman's house can be seen from your front window."

"Yes, it can. Though, of course, I didn't know who lived there until that day."

"Right. Did you by any chance happen to notice if anyone came to his house that day?"

"Oh, I don't pay attention to what the neighbors do. Now, Velda, my neighbor on the right, she doesn't miss a thing."

We thanked Mrs. Klausener and took our leave. As we left the subdivision and drove on Bendtown Road toward the place where I'd been employed for fifteen years, I looked at Shac. "So. Besides the fact that he has no dog so his actions raise suspicion, what are you thinking?"

"I'll get a female undercover officer from Rockville out here to do a 'lawn survey'. She can try to discreetly question Velda, and the other neighbors, to see if anyone noticed a vehicle at Don's house."

"I know a private detective over there. Don might know all the officers on their force."

"The one I have in mind is new. Hired a few weeks ago."

If she was that new, I wondered how Shac knew her, but I was not about to ask. "He must have been ticked off that the neighbor saw him sneaking back home."

"Shouldn't have been surprised though, he would have had to come out of the woods within a few more steps. And cross the street. Plenty of opportunity to be seen."

Thirty-Three

The concrete bulk of Southern Moldings came into view. Shac pulled through the gates and into the parking lot closest to Administration. My security office had been in that section. We stopped at the security window just inside the doors and Shac again displayed his badge.

"What can we do for you, Detective?" The young clean-shaven guy on duty looked about fifteen years old.

"Need to see Maxie Filner. Is she in?"

"As far as I know. I'll page her to come out here. You can wait in that room over there."

"Thanks."

We walked over to the small room nearby, really just an alcove, and sat. We waited for about ten minutes before the inner door opened and Maxie came through. She looked at the young guard, he pointed toward us and shrugged. When she saw me, a look of alarm passed across her face.

We stood up and I let Shac do the talking. It was his show. I hated that Maxie probably thought I had betrayed her. I'd try to explain when this was over. That she knew nothing whatever about the attack on me, I was as certain of as I was of Shac's integrity.

"Cam? What? Nothing's wrong with one of my kids?"

"No, Maxie. I should have known that would be your first thought and had James to say it was not personal." I indicated Shac. "You know Shac, of course."

"Ms. Filner, I'm sorry for your alarm, too. I need to ask you a few routine questions about one of our Wexler Bend detectives, Don Mears."

"What about Don? Is he okay? I haven't seen him for a few months."

"Don was fine when I saw him last evening, Maxie." I told her.

"Did you two break up?" Shac asked.

"I guess. He stopped calling." She hesitated. "I didn't know why. Still don't."

"When did he stop calling?"

"Around New Years, I guess. I was very busy at work and then I realized he hadn't called in a while. So I called him, just to touch base. He was evasive, hardly talked. I hung up. And haven't talked to him since."

I had to made a conscious effort not to catch Shac's eye. New Years. When Oliver connected with Selena. But what connection was there between Oliver and Mears? And how did Vivian come into the picture?

"Do you remember if Mears ever mentioned knowing Vivian Taggert?"

Maxie shook her head. "She was Mr. Taggert's and your ex-wife's..." Her voice trailed off. "Mr. Taggert's daughter, wasn't she?"

"Yes. She was."

"I never heard him mention her."

"How about Selena Goren?"

"The other girl who was killed?"

"Yes."

"He never mentioned her either."

Maxie stared at Shac for a moment. "I thought Don was your partner?"

"That's true," he said.

"So why are you asking these questions about him? It almost sounds like you suspect him of having something to do with the deaths of those girls."

"We've just discovered some information we don't understand."

"Have you asked him about it?"

"We will. Yes. In the meantime, Maxie, if you should see him, please don't mention that we were asking questions."

She looked at her watch. "I really need to get back to work. I told my supervisor I'd use my break to talk to you."

"Of course, if you have a problem, let me know. Thanks for talking to us"

Maxie went back through the door to the building proper. We thanked the security guard and went outside before discussing our talk with Maxie.

"She's your friend. Think she knows anything?"

"No. If she did she'd say so. She wouldn't want to, but she would."

"Why do you think he broke up with her?"

When I didn't answer right away, he stopped beside his car. "Cam? You have an idea why?"

"Unlock the door." I reached for the door handle.

He clicked the remote and we got in, but he didn't start the engine. Waited.

"In January Maxie called to ask if I could loan her a couple hundred dollars. Said she'd had some unexpected expenses for the kids. She paid me back when she got her tax refund."

"And January is when Mears stopped calling." He struck the steering wheel. "You think he borrowed from her and didn't repay?"

"Maybe. Gamblers take money from any source they can. Would even sell their own..." I broke off, hearing my own words.

"'Mothers,' the saying is," Shac finished. "And that's what we're investigating, selling human beings."

He laid his head on the wheel. "How could I not sense something? We've been partners since he made detective. And according to the records, he'd been in deep shit long before then."

"Name someone in the department who'd have believed it. He's popular, well-liked. Ever since he joined the force. You said so."

He started the car and drove out of the parking lot. "And we still haven't found the link, if there is one, between Mears and Oliver."

"My gut says there is one."

"Tell me why your gut says so."

I stared through the windshield, marshalling my thoughts, not seeing the passing landscape. Even the numerous white dogwood trees, a favorite of mine, which had begun to make a comeback from the blight that almost wiped them out a few years ago.

"I never would have imagined him having anything to do with all this until you found his fingerprints on the stuff in my tote bag. Didn't want to then, as you know. To think Don Mears would hit me in the head with a rock just didn't compute."

"Yeah. He always seemed to like you."

"Maybe he somehow got in debt to Marcus Oliver, who will throw anybody under the bus. And Oliver forced him to get involved in whatever he's in, the drugs or trafficking. Or both."

"But Oliver's having cash flow problems, too. The money he gave the guy to stage the fight didn't come from his bank balance. It's nearly bottomed out. He hasn't had a paying legal client in months, according to Louise. So where did it come from? He can't touch the principal in the trust his father set up."

So he'd talked to Louise about her partner. I wondered how much he'd told her. "Vivian had just reached the age that she could access her trust, though."

"So he really needed her alive, and in love with him. What happened to change that?"

I realized I had a glimmering of what might have changed. "Selena Goren's death happened. And he lost the drugs. If he'd already paid for them, he was out the money himself. If he didn't have that much cash available, he was in even more trouble. Presumably he had the wad of cash Selena had on her. But it wouldn't last forever."

"So he was with Vivian the next day for her birthday, getting closer to her and her money. And on Friday she winds up dead in Georgia. And Friday night he's involved in a fake fight to account for some facial bruises. Damn, we have to get his DNA. The GBI lab has to get some trace from her hands. If it matches Oliver we've got him for her death."

"And if it matches the trace from Selena's hands, for her death, too." I said.

"But what about Robert Goren's death?" He scowled. "How does it fit in? Or does it? If Mears shot him with your gun, why? Of course, once he shot him, he had to get rid of the body so he staged the suicide and car accident. Then was seen by Mrs. Krausner sneaking back home."

"The thing three people in the case have in common is money troubles. Goren, Oliver, Mears. Peddling drugs can be a lucrative temptation for somebody who needs money. So how did they connect?"

Shac looked at me. "Mears and Goren through the activity that got them in trouble in the first place, probably. Gambling. Goren would have been exposed and fired soon. He'd embezzled money from his employer. Oliver? Maybe he came into the picture because he knew people who loan money. When the lendee can't pay it back, and gamblers almost never can, they force them to perform services for them."

"He's the one who posed as Selena's boyfriend, we're sure, and intended to sell her to the traffickers. After using her to transport drugs," I said.

"I checked back on calls from the Clare View. Mears was the responding officer on a call to the bar last year when Oliver was being drunk and obnoxious. Report said he talked him into going home peacefully. Hotel didn't want a big ruckus, of course."

I continued the narrative. "So that's how they connected. Mears offered to run interference for Oliver, for a price. He needed money to feed his gambling habit."

"And they need him to stay in the clear. A pipeline into the police department."

"Through us, as friends of Taylor and Jake, he could keep a finger on what the task force was doing."

Shack's grimace told me he'd already figured that out.

"If it was him driving that squad car that drove along Branch Road while I was waiting for you, he had to have recognized my car. But I guess he was afraid to try and silence me again."

"A little late, too. You'd called it in."

Thirty-Four

I saw we'd arrived back at police headquarters. Time to start doing what I said I'd do, look at video files.

We met Taylor in the detective's squad room. She waved us over with a piece of paper. "We finally caught a break. Vivian's other shoe has been found on Clare Creek Mountain."

Shac pumped his fist in the air. "How? Where?"

She grinned. "In a crow's nest."

"What?"

"It's very light weight, with several shiny gemstones set in the straps. I guess they attracted the crow, he picked it up and flew up to his nest. There was a small windstorm passed across the mountain last night, blew the nest down."

"Positive ID as its being Vivian's?"

"Yes. I took it to Louise Taggert's office to show her personally. She confirmed it."

I wondered if Shac would have preferred to be the one to take the sandal to show Louise. Then chastised myself for the thought. What did it matter? I had no romantic claim on him.

"So we have another definite tie to her being abducted on the mountain. And taken to Georgia, where she died," Shac said.

"And another tie-in. Not as definitive. Since Cam hadn't deposited the two hundred dollar bills Selena gave her, we found another in the same series in the cash register of that convenience store in Georgia. The owner kept it because he doesn't get many. It also tested positive for heroin residue. Though that's not unusual."

I thought Taylor still had more to say, and I was right. "That's not all. Something on the surveillance footage from the building across the street from the store."

"Well, give. We're due some breaks," Shac ordered.

"The guy who passed the C-note. Owner picked him out. He wore a hoodie and a cap pulled down low. But a little bit of face showed. Enough to indicate he had a big bruise on his face."

I caught my breath. Her killer. Maybe.

Taylor hesitated. Then said, "He did something a little odd."

"Odd? What?"

"Just as he walked into camera range, leaned against a post, coughing. Held his hand up to his face for a minute, then walked on out of the picture."

"A cold?" Shac said.

I'm sure he thought what I did. Maybe the SOB would get pneumonia and die, but not before he was tried for Vivian's murder.

"It's all coming together. I hope. Where do I go to start looking at footage here, Taylor?"

"That corner over there." She pointed. "The computer's already set up. The guys will be glad to share the disks, I'm sure. Thanks, Cam."

As I walked away Shac said, "I'll fill her in on our interviews with Klausner and Filner. Get her thoughts on them."

"Hope I can find something to help catch the bastards." I went over and spoke to two guys staring intently at monitors as scenes outside our convenience store on Branch Drive flickered across their screens. I recognized one as a Wexler Bend new hire. The other I thought was one of their IT guys. They nodded and the IT guy pushed a stack of high-capacity disks toward me.

I inserted one and the program waited for me to push the arrow telling it to start the video. I clicked on it. According to the time stamp I was viewing footage from a camera inside the store which was recorded at four-fifteen, last Wednesday.

Images flickered past my eyes. People who either didn't care to pay with their cards at the pumps or preferred paying with cash came in and paid for their gas before pumping, as the instructions told them. Some with cash, some with cards, either debit or credit. Some seemed to have trouble communicating with the female clerk, who as I recalled, was a native of India with a heavy accent. I wondered if Taylor had ever talked to her, found out if she remembered seeing anything out of the ordinary on the day of Selena's death. From my observation it would be highly unlikely. Her attention seemed fixed on something under the counter.

Suddenly my finger clicked the mouse pointer to freeze the picture. Don Mears swaggered through the door. There was no other way to describe the way he entered. I touched the mouse again to start the video moving.

Mears did not acknowledge the clerk behind the counter. Walked over to the candy aisle where he chose a Milky Way candy bar, peeled the wrapper and began eating. He paced along the aisle for a few minutes, looked at his watch. The bell over the door must have sounded, he looked toward it.

Another man joined him in the aisle. Marcus Oliver. They touched hands but it did not look like a handshake. Oliver had handed Mears something. Maybe when IT enhanced the picture it would show up. I let the video run until Mears was out of the picture, made note of the time stamp. Oliver remained. Was he meeting someone else?

Then a woman was running up to him, touched his arm, smiled. Not a woman, Selena Goren. She had met him there. I could hardly believe my hunch was proving to be fact. I started to call Shac and Taylor. Then I noticed that Oliver didn't seem too happy to see her. He brushed her arm away. She said a few words and he handed her a bill, then walked hurriedly out of the picture toward the door. Selena went to the register and and handed the bill to the clerk then she left.

I made note of the numbers immediately after Selena left. I wanted to rerun it, but called Shac instead.

"I think you and Taylor will want to see this."

He wasted no time getting across the room, trailed by Taylor. By the time they reached my desk I'd backed up the video to where Don Mears arrived. They and the other two video watchers crowded around me.

When it had run to the part where Selena and Oliver left, I stopped it again. Shac asked me to run it again and stop where Oliver handed Mears whatever he did. He asked the IT guy if he thought if it would show what was handed off if it was enhanced, blown up. The guy shrugged, replied that they'd just have to try and see.

We watched it again, this time running it past the place I'd stopped previously. But nothing else of interest showed to the end of that disk. Taylor handed it to the IT guy and requested copies. "If anything happens to this disk, your ass is mine." She smiled, but I got the feeling she meant every word.

As the guy walked away to make the copies, she squeezed my shoulder. "I do believe this will be enough that a judge will sign off on an order to compel a DNA sample." She exulted as she pulled out her phone.

Unfortunately Taylor must have forgotten who we were after. No local judge could be located. They were tied up, unable to see her, out of town or had left strict orders not to be disturbed for any reason. I kept looking at video footage along with the new-hire patrolman. Even with peripheral vision I could pick up Taylor's frustration increasing exponentially. I couldn't blame her.

I heard a grunt from my companion across the desk. "I think this is that same guy."

I froze my video and walked around behind him. A small, maybe black, sports car was pulled up close to the building .The patrolman said he'd backed it up to just before a second vehicle came into the picture. A second or two after he restarted the video, a late model Toyota Prius pulled up beside the building on the side where I'd first noticed the cameras. Someone left the Prius on the passenger side, got in the sports car and drove off. The Prius then left also.

"It is, indeed. You've passed your sharp eye test." I patted him and called Shac and Taylor back over. Just as they reached us the IT guy came back and handed Taylor several disks.

"Hang around, we may have more to be duped," she told him.

We watched the Prius arrive and leave again. Taylor silently removed the disk and handed it over to IT. He gave a half-grin and said, "I know. My ass."

"Guess I'll have to call in the big guns. None of your excellent local jurists are willing to take the risk of signing off on justice for our throwaway girls."

"A federal judge?" I asked.

"Yes. But I'd better take it to the circuit level. I'll fly to Nashville."

When IT returned with the duplicate disks he took them to Taylor and came back to our corner.

I stretched and looked at my watch. "Guys, I vote we take a break and get some lunch. We can get back to it in a half hour."

"Suits me." They both agreed.

We stood up just as Shac came through the door bearing several pizza boxes. He motioned for us to follow him. We trooped into the break room and found seats. Shac had brought three containers of tea along with the pizza. "Dig in," he invited.

We devoured pizza and our drinks, then rose as one to go back to our videos. You'd have thought we were watching our favorite action flicks. Nothing like a taste of success to reinvigorate a team.

Thirty-Five

We finished the convenience store video for that day. The next group of disks was Saturday video from the two cameras above the lower parking lot near the dam on Clare Creek Mountain. The first parts went fast, a lot of dark nothing. After daylight we saw squirrels, birds, other wild life scampering around looking for breakfast. At nine-thirty a.m., by the time stamp, a black sports car drove into the lot and parked near the path leading to the dam. A path I remembered well.

I stopped breathing almost. Marcus Oliver got out of the car that I had been sure belonged to him when it entered the lot. He walked up through the lot and out of the picture. I had no idea where the next camera might pick him up. I continued watching my disk. No one else was about in the park at this early hour. Or at least in the parking lot. Shuttle buses began their round trips at nine o'clock, when the park opened, but they took passengers to the artifact exhibit building. Vivian had already arrived, as video from the shuttle had shown.

Nothing else happened until about half an hour later. Vivian and Oliver walked into the picture, holding hands. They continued walking to the path to the dam. Vivian turned her face up and in a shockingly quick move, Oliver's fist slammed into her chin. I jumped and exclaimed, "Son of a bitch!"

My fellow watchers looked up and Shac, who was approaching us, said, "What the hell was that about, Cam?"

"See for yourself. Has Taylor left?"

He nodded. "Her chopper took off forty-five minutes ago. Didn't check with the tower, but they saw it."

"You'll have to send this to her phone. It'll cinch the request for an order to compel."

At that moment his phone rang. When he answered I could hear Tawson's voice clearly. "Lane. Get in here. Bring Locke."

We took off. Tawson had sounded as though two seconds would be too long. When we reached his doorway, he said, "Shut the door."

Shac closed it and we stood waiting. "The chopper carrying Taylor Glass and her pilot went down on the Cumberland Plateau ten minutes ago. Fatalities unknown. But you know the terrain, we can probably assume she did not survive."

I rocked back, then sat down, uninvited. Shac stood, unmoving. Taylor. Always perfectly groomed Taylor Glass. Dead. I could not take it in.

"How..." Shac stopped, swallowed and started again. "How did you find out?"

"A plane carrying Sergeant Jake Hunter along with two federal Marshals was just landing at Tri-County when he got the call from the Task Force Commander. Search parties are being dispatched, but brace for the worst."

"Marshals?" Shac and I exchanged puzzled looks.

"They have come to arrest Marcus Oliver and deliver him into the custody of the Georgia Bureau of Investigation. The GBI will hold him until a determination is made as to the jurisdiction in which he will be tried for the murder of Vivian Taggert."

"Captain, I'm glad he'll be charged for her murder. But how did it come about?"

"Taylor Glass sent all the evidence we had accumulated, including the sandal found on Clare Creek Mountain, to the GBI. Fortunately, Federal Circuit judges are not in fear of our Tennessee judges. An order was issued forcing the release of Marcus Oliver's DNA evidence from the assault case in Nashville. There was a match to trace collected from Vivian Taggert's body."

Shac told him, "We'd better share the video from the camera in the park of him punching her out. It will cinch their case."

"You found it?"

"Just had when you called."

"Good. But I also want him, and anyone else involved, for our case. His attorneys are filing motions and requests for suppression of evidence left and right."

I was sure of that. "The surveilance video of him meeting Selena at the convenience store places him with her near the time of her death," I blurted.

"Indeed. I expect my department to uncover more evidence." His powerful jaw worked for a moment. "And I want the bad apple in my department removed, legally and without recourse."

"Yes, sir." Shac's voice was hard as steel.

This was too convenient. I wanted to know something. I figured he wouldn't know, but he could find out. "Captain Tawson?"

Tawson looked at me without saying anything.

"Were there any witnesses to the crash?"

"No. Pilot radioed Cookeville Tower that his engine was stalling. He was going to try to land in a clearing he could see. That's the last they heard."

I pushed my luck. "Did anyone here know Jake and the Marshals were coming with a warrant to arrest Oliver?"

"No one, not even me."

"And was their regular pilot flying the chopper?"

He stared for a moment. "I don't know." He picked up the phone and called his more-or-less counterpart with airport security. He asked the question, then waited a couple of minutes.

He hung up, his face expressionless.

"No one knows. The chopper pilot didn't check in with the tower before takeoff or file a flight plan, as required, even for TBI aircraft. Their pilot usually hangs around the airport in case he's needed, but no one's seen him for a while so they assumed he was the one flying the chopper. Is she clairvoyant, Lane?"

Shac gave copies of the disks with the incriminating images of our suspects to Captain Tawson and we left the station. As we stood on the sidewalk a squad car pulled up in front. Jake and, I assumed, the Marshals got out.

"Jake. Glad Georgia's on the ball. We'll get our turn at the SOB." Shac said.

Jake just nodded.

After they'd gone in I said to Shac, "I guess they took him in through the sally port?"

"They didn't look very happy. But this is probably just a courtesy call on Captain Tawson and the Chief."

"Where's Don?" I realized I hadn't seen him since his late-night call at my house.

"Good question. He didn't come in today. Or call in."

I whirled around. "You don't know where he is?"

"BOLO out. We'll find him."

"Or not." I whispered. "Don Mears has a pilot's license, doesn't he?"

He jerked around to look at me. "Yes, he does. Are you clairvoyant, Cam? I'm on my way to the airport to see if anyone has seen him. Coming?"

We started with people working near the hangar where the TBI helicopter was kept. After we'd talked to half a dozen workers, the driver of a luggage buggy told us he thought the guy flying the TBI chopper when it took off did look like Don Mears. And he thought, but wasn't sure, that a woman was in a back seat. He wasn't positive, but it was enough for us.

While we were at the airport Shac got a call. The TBI pilot had been found in a field behind the airport, alive, barely. He would not be flying again soon, if ever. The good news, for us, at least, was that just maybe Taylor was alive. My money was on her. Since Mears, if it was he flying the chopper, had apparently decided not to take her out immediately in a preemptive strike.

What puzzled me was why. Did he think she carried the only copy of the evidence? Or was it a ploy to get clean away? He knew he would be identified as the pilot. But in the rugged terrain on the Plateau, a body might never be found. He would most likely be assumed to be dead, so eventually they would stop looking.

Then I noticed the look on Shac's face. If he squeezed his phone any harder he would have to invest in a new one. "What?"

"They didn't get Oliver." He spoke so quietly I would have preferred if he had roared.

"Say what? Why not?" My own voice climbed an octave or two.

"He wasn't at his home. Or anywhere else they looked."

"Is he on the chopper with Mears and Taylor?"

"Most likely. Unless they've landed. Or did crash."

We walked out of the terminal. I couldn't forget Taylor. Was she still alive? We weren't best friends. But I liked and respected her. She was fully capable of holding her own in most any situation. But being in the clutches of two cold-blooded killers was a bad situation.

Thirty-Six

After we were in Shac's car I remembered something I'd intended to ask him. "You explained why Taylor joined the TBI. She shot a terrorist and saved a State Department Attache. Is she really good with a gun?"

"Very. Some might say she's obsessed with weapons."

"Why's that?"

He drove up to the exit gate, tossed a dollar to the attendant. To discourage them from taking up premium space in front of the terminal, the airport didn't charge cops for parking, but Shac always paid. "Actually obsessed with finding ways to carry one undetectably. Did you ever see her weapon?"

Now that I thought about it, I hadn't. And on the rare occasions I noticed her with a purse, it was extremely small.

"From her time with the State Department. Idiots frowned on guns, even carried by Security. Claimed the military details assigned was all they needed. That's always worked so well, what with the military guards' hands, or weapons, hamstrung with regulations."

"So. You think she has a chance even with those two?"

"They probably would rather not kill a TBI agent, especially a Task Force member. Mears, at least, knows they'd have extra crosshairs on their backs forever. Even bottom-feeders like traffickers would just dispose of the two responsible for bringing on that much scrutiny, and leave their bodies to be found."

I felt a little easing of worry for Taylor.

"Of course, there's a scenario that could avoid that." He merged with traffic on the Interstate and didn't say anything else.

"You might as well lay it on me. I'll imagine the worst anyway."

"If they put parachutes on and jumped. Even put one on Taylor and tapped her on the head so she didn't jump and went down with the chopper."

"But they'd still be guilty of killing a TBI agent," I protested.

"They radioed Cookeville their engine conked out. Oliver's a lawyer. That could lay the groundwork for a defense if they were ever caught."

I didn't say anything until we left the Interstate and were almost back at headquarters. If Taylor was still alive, where was she right now? I couldn't accept that she might be dead. She was so alive, so take charge. With her training I had to believe that she was going to make it back.

"God, I don't want to face Jake." Shac said. "There has to be another leak. How else did they know things were closing in?"

"Yes, there is," I said slowly, "but not from here."

"What do you mean?"

"Oliver, Senior has been around a long time. Has a lot of friends and people who owe him. Not just in Tennessee."

Shac looked through the windshield. "He couldn't manage to get a Federal court order out of Georgia squashed, when he was tipped off about it. But he could warn his son."

"You're always telling me to ditch the guilt. It keeps you from seeing the big picture. Let's go find Jake."

We went inside and through to the squad room. Jake was seated at the desk where I'd stared at video files earlier. He was looking blankly at the monitor as the video feed scrolled across. We sank into nearby chairs in silence. I wasn't sure if he was aware of us.

"Don't let the mother or Nathan Taggert see these," he said, without looking around.

"No, we won't," Shac said.

"Judge Oliver once had a long-term relationship with a female judge in Dahlonegah. She's with a Federal judge on the North Georgia Circuit now. We can't prove he was given information or that he tipped off his son."

When he finally looked around at us the pain that his voice didn't betray was clearly visible in his eyes. I could stop imagining that his feelings for me were more than deep-rooted friendship. He was certain Taylor was dead and could hardly bear it.

"Where are the Marshals?" I finally asked.

"They got rooms for us at the Six. I might as well go, too."

I looked at Shac and tried to get across to him with head motions that he should take Jake home with him. He finally got it and said, "Come on, you can bunk at my place."

"I'm not fit company for anybody, even the Marshals. I'll probably sit in a coffee shop all night."

"Works for me." Shac said.

"I'm going home for a few minutes, make sure the workmen locked up," I said. "Then I'll join you." No need to ask where they'd be. There was only one all-night coffee shop in Wexler Bend.

I drove home more slowly than usual. Remembered Don Mears driving Shac and me to my house and finding the Task Force there. I touched the side of my head, now healed enough it didn't need a bandage. Mears had been the one responsible for the damage and neither Shac or I had a clue.

When I reached my street and saw my house, I gulped. It was a glaring island of light. I'd joked to Shac that I'd piss my neighbors off with so much light. In fact, it might not be a joke. Oh well, there were bound to be on and off switches for them. Or maybe some kind of rheostat to dial down the brightness. I hoped.

I turned in my driveway, then saw the car parked on the gravelled area. *De ja vu, Taylor*, I thought, with a catch in my throat. It reminded me of returning from my errands and seeing Selena's Infiniti backed up in the gravel. So she could leave in a hurry. As I now knew, she'd driven to the service station on Branch Road. And then to her death by the river. Don't think about that now.

This was Nathan Taggert's yellow Jeep, I realized with relief. Even so I parked in my usual spot and waited until he emerged. I opened my door and got out, hand inside my bag on my Glock.

"Cam, it's just me. I'm sorry, but I had to see if you could tell me anything. I heard on the news –"

"Let's go inside, Nathan." I cut him off and pulled out my keys. We went in and I closed and locked the door and reset the alarm.

Thirty-Seven

I must have been transmitting some uneasy vibrations. "It's true then? The police were about to arrest somebody and they escaped?"

"What was on the news?"

"Not much. That there may be two suspects and they got away. One source told the station they may have escaped by plane."

"That's about all I can tell you, Nathan. I'm sorry."

"They also said there was a rumor that an officer of a state police agency may be missing, possibly a hostage."

God, where did the stations get their information? Maybe a low-level clerk who wanted to appear 'in-the-know.'

"That is pure speculation. The police will release information when it's the right time." I spoke more sharply than I meant to and immediately regretted it. Nathan had just lost a daughter and I seemed to be the only person other than his Twelve Step group that he could talk to about it. And that thought reminded me I'd missed her funeral. The funeral was probably why his face looked so drawn, his complexion had a grayish pallor. Grief and guilt are a really bad combination, I knew well.

"Nathan, I am so sorry. I was going to be at Vivian's funeral. But I went with Shac to a couple interviews with people." I just caught myself before mentioning the videos. I finished lamely. "And other investigation stuff."

"It's okay, Cam. I saw your beautiful red lilies. I know I've been a pest."

"No, no. Would you like some coffee?"

"Sure. But I don't want to cause you trouble."

"No trouble. I always have the Bunn ready. As Shac says, I mainline the stuff."

My tote bag was still on my shoulder as I went to the kitchen to hit the switch on the coffee maker. I shoved it inside a cabinet and hoped I'd remember doing it. Since my gun was in it, I was hesitant to leave it in a room with Nathan in his present state of mind. One of my guns in the wrong hands was one too many already.

I pulled a couple of mugs from the dishwasher, which I still hadn't unloaded. Another reminder of the night Taylor and Jake convened the task force here rather than haul me down to headquarters with a head injury.

I started to turn and take the mugs of coffee to the living room and Nathan was right behind me. A little coffee slopped on my hand. He grabbed a paper towel and dried it. "I'm sorry. I'm sorry. Is your hand burned?"

"No. It's fine." I handed a mug to him and headed back to the living room. Why had he followed me to the kitchen? Had he seen me put my tote bag in the cabinet? I'd keep my eye on him.

I took my usual easy chair and he dropped on the sofa again.

"Will her killer be caught?" His question caught me off guard. Would they? I was convinced now that Don Mears was involved in both deaths. How I wasn't sure. But I knew Shac wouldn't stop looking until he found Mears and Oliver. Nor Jake. Jake, especially, as I knew now. How long had he been in love with her? When did they meet? I realized Nathan was still talking.

"Her mother finally returned my call right after the funeral. She asked all kinds of questions. Who did the police suspect? Why was Vivian in Georgia? As though she'd ever cared."

"Maybe on some level, I guess. Surely. She's her mother."

"She didn't want a child. I convinced her to keep the baby when we found out she was pregnant."

I didn't know what to say, so kept quiet. He probably needed to let it out.

His words brought up something I'd never really considered. What would I do if I ever found I was pregnant?

184

Not likely, with my job and the time constaints it imposed. Not to mention my contacts mainly consisted of people with the same irregular lifestyles, such as law enforcement and others in my profession. I didn't think that I was a prime candidate for motherhood. But I didn't think I could destroy a child before birth, either. So that would leave two choices. Put the child up for adoption or raise him or her, both of us learning as we went. To my surprise I realized that the second option was probably the choice I would make.

"Did Vivian hate her mother?" I asked the question before I realized I was going to ask it.

"No. I think she cut her more slack than I could. Especially as she got older, wanted her own life, too. Did you hate your mother?"

Startled, I realized I should have seen that coming. Before I could answer though my doorbell rang. Had Jake and Shac come to check on me since I hadn't joined them at the coffee shop? Or called, either, I realized belatedly.

When I looked through my peephole I saw that Louise Taggert and Shac were standing in the glare of one of my new security lights. What in the hell? He was supposed to be with Jake. Not his ex-wife.

I opened the door as Nathan came to stand beside me. He stood and stared at the two people on my doorstep.

Thirty-Eight

"What did I tell you, Shac?" Louise Taggert pointed an accusing finger at her most recent ex-husband.

"Hell, Louise. What of it? You're not married to him anymore."

I wanted to pound Shac, kick him out in the yard. "You mean you brought her to my house to see if her other ex-husband was here? Why, for God's sake?"

I fell back or Louise would have mowed me down as she stormed in without invitation. "Are you all right, Nathan?" She took his arm and led him back to the couch.

His sad face was now a picture of bewilderment. "Well, of course. Why wouldn't I be? And why are you here?"

"This – this supposed private investigator tries to move in on vulnerable men. You can't be taken in by her fake sympathy?"

"I don't know what you're after, Louise. I was waiting for Cam when she got home. I needed to talk to someone, find out if it was true that Vivian's murderer had escaped before being arrested."

"Like I said, you're vulnerable. You just lost Vivian and are lost in grief. I'll take you home with me."

Fury he'd probably never shown before filled Nathan's eyes. "Take me home with you? I don't think so. Not when it's your law partner who probably killed my girl. Maybe going to sell her to sex traffickers."

Her small eyes opened wide in shock, "Nathan. How can you say that?"

"Because they were dating. Did you know that?"

"That can't be true. And even if they were dating, he wouldn't do that." But her voice trailed off, as though something had occurred to her.

Shac and I had stood in the middle of the floor listening to this exchange. Now our eyes met, with a question in them. What did Louise know? Or suspect?

"Did Oliver tell you she wanted those red sandals? The ones you gave her because you wanted to ingratiate yourself into her life? For her inheritance?"

"No, Nathan. You've got it all wrong. I always loved Vivian. I – "

He was inexorable. "And now you're trying to worm your way back into my life because you know I'll inherit her trust? I know money's the reason you married me in the first place. Because my father was Board Chairman of Eastern."

She touched a tissue to nonexistent tears. "I can't believe you think that. But why do you think this – this woman is befriending you?"

"I've no idea. I wouldn't blame her if she kicked my butt to the sidewalk." He straightened up, his voice sounded strangled with strong emotion. Went to the front door and opened it, reached for the storm door. "Go. I've heard enough of your counterfeit caring."

Suddenly the storm door handle was yanked from Nathan's hand, almost pulling him through it. Then he was shoved so hard he fell on the floor several feet from where he had stood. A mocking voice sounded as a man came through in a rush. He slammed the door, without locking the storm door. "How cozy. Why don't we all just settle down and be friends?"

Marcus Oliver stood in my living room, a gun in his hand. "All of you. Get over there on the sofa." He waved the gun to emphasize his words.

Louise wore a look of shock, though not surprise, I noticed. I saw her gather herself to try and talk herself out of this situation. I'm sure she gave no thought as to whether the rest of us would get out alive.

"Marcus? What are you doing here?" She gave a little laugh. "Why do all the men in my life wind up at Cameron Locke's dump?"

"Pretty nice dump for a PI, Louise. Better than the one you'll have after you file for bankruptcy."

"Bankruptcy? Whatever gives you that idea? You and I have made a good team. Our business will pick up."

"Really, Louise? You mean it won't matter if my father isn't able to keep me from being convicted of murder in Georgia?"

His cackle of laughter had a manic note to it. Coming from a face that was still multi-colored, black, blue, green and yellow, it was enough to chill a person. I noticed a new bruise, and a large lump on his forehead near the hairline. Just where mine had been. Had Mears put it there? Where was he? Was he the only fugitive on the plane with Taylor when it took off?

"Your father won't let that happen. You know he won't." Louise sounded positive. Did she really believe that?

"His sphere of influence is not that powerful in Georgia. I was lucky he was able to get me a warning the Marshals were coming."

So Jake had been right. That's how he knew to cut out. And where was Jake? I couldn't ask Shac now. And my cell phone was in my tote bag. In the kitchen. Along with my gun.

Oliver dismissed Louise with a shrug. "All right, everyone. Throw your cell phones over in the corner." Louise, Nathan and Shac all tossed their cell phones.

"Now, put your gun on the floor real easy, Shac. Then kick it over to me. Cam, you, too."

I spread my hands. "Don't have a cell phone or gun on me. I'll know better next time."

"What makes you think there'll be a next time? Women. Think they can lord it over men. That black bitch at the hotel is a friend of yours?" He leveled his gun at my chest. I tried to brace myself for a bullet smashing through flesh and bone. It was questionable if I'd feel more than the initial impact. I had no illusions but that I was facing a killer.

"What happened to your partner, Oliver?" Shac asked in a casual tone. "No match for a trained police officer, are you? Just young women no one cares enough about to keep safe."

I heard Nathan's sharp intake of breath. If we lived through this I knew Shac would beg his forgiveness.

"That worthless piece of crap?" That manic laugh again. It triggered a coughing spell. His breathing was ragged.

What was wrong with him? He was losing control. I could feel it.

"He knew how to work the system. Cheated his way through the academy. Then got hooked on gambling. He'd have been dead meat a long time ago, but he was useful, gave us a pipeline so we knew what the police were doing." Another coughing spell.

He waved his gun at me again. "Damn asthma. Water. Get me a glass of water. Anything funny and Lane dies." The gun was now pointed squarely at Shac's chest.

I backed slowly toward the kitchen. "All my glasses are in the dishwasher. I'll have to step over to the side."

"Just get it." He coughed again, harder. "No... or Lane dies," he gasped.

Thirty-Nine

I opened the cabinet, grabbed my gun and whirled just as a bullet shattered my front door lock. Taylor Glass kicked the door in, hitting Oliver squarely and knocking him forward. My bullet tore his throat open. But not before the reflex of his trigger finger got off one shot. I looked down at him, and the irrelevant thought went through my mind that he didn't have to worry about asthma now.

Jake barreled into the room, entering from the hallway. He looked around, saw that the danger, at least from Oliver, was over and lowered his own weapon.

Louise was sitting on the floor, whimpering, holding her shoulder. She paid no attention to Nathan, who lay on his side staring at her, though he would never see her face again. His lips had a faint curve, probably just a dying muscle contraction. But I hoped it was because he was returning the welcoming smile of his daughter.

Taylor was on her cell phone requesting three ambulances. "But only one is urgent." I heard her say.

I presumed she meant the one for Louise. Oliver and Nathan were in no hurry to get to the morgue. When she disconnected she looked at me.

"Nice shot."

"I meant it for his chest. Somebody must have jostled him."

Her mouth curved in a grin, then it faded. Jake walked over to her, touched her shoulder. "You could have caught that bullet."

"Not me. I always break to the side when I breach a doorway. I knew Cam could shoot straight."

I asked, "How could you know? We never got to the range."

"Screensaver?" She nodded toward my home computer.

"Oh. Yeah." The screensaver on both my home and office computers was a series of images of the targets I perforated at the gun club shooting range.

I sat down beside Shac on the sofa. "He only got one shot off. How did they both get hit." I nodded at Louise and Nathan.

"He jumped in front of her. Can you believe that?"

"Yes. I can. He was a decent guy."

"Yeah." He looked at me. "Why in hell was your bag in the kitchen? You never leave it in the kitchen."

I made a face. "When I got home Nathan was waiting for me. I was jumpy. And he seemed so despondent. We came in and I went to get coffee. I didn't want to leave it, with my gun inside, in the room with him so I stuck it in a cabinet."

He just shook his head.

"Are you going to let me bleed to death, Shac? After your skank of a girlfriend almost got me shot point blank?" Louise had regained some of her arrogance, even through her whining.

"Know any first aid, Taylor?" Shac asked.

"Not much," she said.

Shac looked at me. "Cam can tie a mean tourniquet. Remember when I sliced an artery trying to fix a hose on your heap a couple years ago?"

"A tourniquet for a shoulder wound? Are you nuts?" I shook my head, miming amazement at his total ineptitude.

"She's not touching me. Stay away from me, you killer." Louise shouted.

She was saved from any tender ministrations from me or Taylor by the arrival of an ambulance, sirens wide open. I could hear several police cars advertising their imminent arrival close behind the ambulance. Well, my new neighbors had had a year of peace after I arrived in their midst. I guess the honeymoon was over.

Louise was taken to the hospital, after the flesh wound in her shoulder was bandaged, none too gently, I noticed, by the paramedic. She never stopped complaining and claimed she needed something for pain. He gave her a shot of something with what looked like a veterinarian's needle.

My living room was taken over by crime scene techs. All of us were questioned separately for what seemed like hours by Captain Tawson, Shac's immediate boss, Commander Calendula, and one of Taylor's superiors out of Knoxville. It was all routine, had to be done, even though it didn't seem right to me. After all we had all nearly lost our lives in taking down two killers. Shac, Jake and Taylor took it more or less in stride. Maybe I should count my blessings that I hadn't made it into the police force.

At last the questioning was done. The bodies of Nathan and Oliver had been taken away to the morgue, where they would undergo autopsies. Our questioners were gone, presumably to write up pages and pages of reports. When the son of a highly placed jurist in the state was one of those killed and suspected of being a killer, all i's had to be dotted, all t's crossed. The video evidence should make it easier.

My living room was covered with detritus from the paramedics, splinters from the door Taylor had kicked in, and copious bloodstains. When our interrogators finally left, and we were free, I grabbed my tote bag from the cabinet in the kitchen and led the way down the side hall.

Forty

The sun's rays were just slanting through my office windows when the four of us entered. When I saw that my office door was still in one piece, I looked a question at Jake.

"I picked the lock. Before Taylor went around to the front. She really wanted to be the one to take down Oliver."

"Sorry." I said.

"But not really, huh?" Her smile was grim.

"Not really," I agreed. "And you got to get Mears. Which, by the way..."

She raised a perfect eyebrow. "How?"

"I know you've told your story until you're sick of telling it. But Shac and I want to know, too."

"Before she gets into that, I think we all need some liquid sustenance. Do you have anything, Locke?" Shac was rummaging through file cabinets, my small office refrigerator.

"Geez. You're getting everything out of place. Here it is." I reached behind a fake book and pulled out a bottle of Kahlua. "I turned on the coffee, it'll be ready in a minute."

Jake was pulling cups, spoons and sugar from drawers in the credenza. I went over and sat beside Taylor on the settee under the window.

She grinned. "They're handy, aren't they?"

I smiled back. "Yes, they are."

When I didn't glance away but kept looking at her, she said, "What?"

"I'm glad you're not dead."

"All things considered, so am I." She crossed one knee over the other. For once her clothing was not pristine. A large grease spot adorned the left leg of her khaki pants. I found that reassuring.

Shac handed us steaming cups, the coffee deliciously flavored with Kahlua. We sipped.

"All right. Give."

"I'd gotten word that Jake and the Marshals were on their way. I didn't want to take a chance the two scumbags would get away. When Mears ambushed me on stakeout at Oliver's place, I thought it was all over. For me anyway. I knew they were merciless."

She looked around the room. "I'm taking the old man down, too, if it takes my whole lifetime." I believed her.

She continued. "He dragged me over to Oliver's car, put my own handcuffs on me and Oliver drove to the private hangar at the airport where we keep the TBI chopper when it's here. They put me on board and handcuffed me to the seat. Mears started the engine, stopped and opened the door. Oliver asked him what he was doing. Mears hit him on the head with his gun, then kicked him out the door.

"He noticed my surprise and laughed. 'He's too much of a liability now. His old man wants him gone. I can't shoot him with my gun and I don't have Locke's anymore. I'll let whoever catches up to him do it.' His exact words."

"So he did shoot Goren with my gun."

"That's how I took it." She drank more coffee.

"He strapped on a parachute then and took off, headed southwest, by the position of the sun. He flew so low sometimes I thought we'd catch on the tree tops. While he concentrated on the flying I was working at getting the handcuffs off. I guess he wanted to brag. He asked if I wanted to know what he was going to do with me. I said I did, that I didn't think he wanted to kill a TBI agent.

"He laughed, said he wouldn't care but knew they'd never stop looking for him. But he didn't tell me what he had planned."

She got up and carried her cup over to the aquarium. "We were over the Cumberland by then. He radioed the nearest airport tower that his engine was stuttering, trying to go out. He was going to to try and set it down.

"I knew there were some deep lakes up there. I thought maybe he was going to jump out and let the chopper crash in one with me in it. So I figured I better get those cuffs off pretty quick. Finally managed to do it but kept my hands down so he didn't see. By then he had set us down in a pasture."

She came back to the settee, patting Jake's shoulder on the way. From the look in her eyes Jake's feelings were reciprocated.

"He said 'End of the ride for you, Glass, have to give you the same love tap I gave Locke, leave you for the bears.' He opened the door and climbed down. Then reached in the back to take the cuff from the seat, I guess, and pull me out.

"I'd got my hand on my hidden weapon. He realized I was free and grabbed his gun, but the parachute straps slowed him down. I had to shoot him through my good pants." Her index finger poked through a hole I hadn't noticed in her waist band.

"Shac told me about your obsession with hidden weapons. But how did you get those cuffs off?" I asked.

She spread out the fingers of her right hand. "A while back I was looking at my Academy ring, all its edges and protuberances. So I did some creative work on it, to conceal a makeshift cuff key. You never know."

"And then?"

"Well, I couldn't leave his body there for the bears, like he planned for me. Believe me, it wasn't easy getting him back in that chopper though. He'd set it down a little close to the forest. Lucky for me I guess he wasn't a real good pilot, so had to keep his attention on his flying. I took off and flew back to the airport here."

"So how did you both get to my house?" I asked. "And how did you know Oliver was here?"

"I knew I couldn't take time to explain it all, to airport security and the cops, especially the dead body of a police detective in the chopper. I slipped through the fence and hitchhiked into town. Tracked down Jake at the coffee shop. He was wondering where you were."

She looked at Shac. "We knew the only thing that would have kept you from comforting him for my loss was if Cam needed you." Her smile was sunny. "So we figured you both might need us, too."

Jake finished up the story. "She could see what was happening through a gap in the drapes. We discussed who'd go through the front. And she pulled rank."

ABOUT THE AUTHOR

Sylvia Nickels writes from her home in the foothills of East Tennessee. Several of her novels and some of her short stories are set in that beautiful area. She is a member and webmaster for Lost State Writers Guild, long-time regional writers' group.

Sylvia has published two mystery novel series. *Requiem for a Party Girl*, *Delusion for a Lonely Girl* and *Anguish for a Wounded Girl* feature female private investigator Cameron Locke.

The first book in Sylvia's other mystery series, *Disguise for Death*, features Royce Thorne, and was released by The Wild Rose Press.

For a few years Sylvia wrote a weekly column for a local newspaper called *Life Slices*. A collection of those columns, *Life Slices, A Medley of Musings after Three Score and More*, is available on Amazon and other online venues. Her memoir, *Eight Miles of Muddy Road*, recounts her childhood as a sharecropper's daughter in rural Georgia, and is also available from online venues.

Other books are *Best Served Cold, Revenge a la Carte*, a collection of her short mystery fiction, print/ebook; *Love Comes Home* (under pen name, Mallory Marrs); *Ringer Blues* novelette and *Just Deserts* flash fiction, ebooks.

Connect with Sylvia:
Writing Blog:
http://www.mysterylanerambler.blogspot.com/
Writing website: http:www.ramblinscribe.com

Sylvia's Personal Blog:
http://www.postoakchronicles.blogspot.com
Personal Website:
http://www.sylvianickels.com

FBI website on human trafficking:

Investigations:

FBI human trafficking investigations are conducted by agents within the human trafficking program and members of our federal human trafficking task forces, and every one of our 56 field offices has worked investigations pertaining to human trafficking. Often, investigations involving human trafficking come to the attention of field offices and task forces through:

Citizen complaints;
The National Human Trafficking Resource Center Hotline;
A referral from a law enforcement agency;
A referral from non-government organizations (NGOs);
Proactive victim recovery operations; and
Outreach to state government and community entities.
....

If you believe you are the victim of a trafficking situation or may have information about a potential trafficking situation, call the National Human Trafficking Resource Center (NHTRC) at 1-888-373-7888. NHTRC is a national, toll-free hotline, with specialists available to answer calls from anywhere in the country, 24 hours a day, seven days a week, every day of the year related to potential trafficking victims, suspicious behaviors, and/or locations where trafficking is suspected to occur. You can also submit a tip to the NHTRC online.

https://www.fbi.gov/about-us/investigate/civilrights/human_trafficking

http://traffickingresourcecenter.org/
Tel:888-373-7888